She took a breath to regain control and pushed back just a bit so that she could look at him.

"I really appreciate your understanding. I'm sorry I didn't trust you with this earlier."

Brian reached one hand up to wipe a stray tear from her cheek. "You didn't know you could trust me, especially given the past. I hope you know now that you can."

Justine nodded.

Brian's eyes were locked on hers. His arms still held her close, and even before he lowered his lips to hers, she knew he was going to kiss her. And she knew she wasn't going to pull away.

Chapter One

It looked like something out of a Stephen King novel, Justine Chatry thought, as she stared at the house in front of her in the fading dim of daylight. Of course, *mansion* was a better word for the ten-thousand-square-foot, three-story monstrosity that rose up out of the bayou, its dark windows peeking out from moss-covered stone and seeming to stare back at her.

It was at least eighty degrees in Cypriere, Louisiana, but Justine felt a chill come over her, and she crossed her arms in front of her chest, trying to cast off the feeling of foreboding. laMalediction, the locals called it—meaning "the curse." Both beautiful and horrifying, seductive and sinister, it seemed to call to her.

And that gave her the creeps.

She chided herself for being fanciful and reached back into her car to grab her small suitcase. Just because her mother chose to believe in haunts and curses didn't mean Justine followed suit. The house was a house. Granted, this house was an extremely large one—with a bloody history—but that didn't change the job she had to do. In fact, it made her job all the more interesting.

"You made it." A voice called from the entry to the house, and Justine looked up and waved at Olivia Markham, the woman who'd hired her for the research job at laMalediction. Olivia smiled and crossed the courtyard to Justine's car.

"I'm glad to see you," Olivia said. "I was starting to worry you wouldn't make it here by dark. We've made some strides clearing the road to the house, but it's still not the best place to be at night if you don't know where you're going."

Justine smiled, thinking "road" was a bit of a stretch to call the dirt path almost hidden by the swamp. "Sorry I worried you. I got held up by my mother. She's a professional at making me late."

Olivia opened the door to the backseat and pulled out one of Justine's boxes of supplies. "I hope she's not worried about you staying here," Olivia said, as they walked toward the house.

Justine frowned. "She's not thrilled, but my mother is not your average person."

Olivia balanced the box on her hip and opened the front door to the house so Justine could walk inside. "What do you mean?" Olivia asked. "Is there such a thing as an average mother?"

"Probably not, but mine is worse than most. She was raised deep in the bayou and still believes in the old ways."

Olivia closed the door and stared at her. "Voodoo?"

"Yeah," Justine said and stared beyond Olivia at the wall behind her. Her mother's insistence on using spells and potions to manage every aspect of her life and health, along with her attempts to direct Justine the same way, had resulted in years of constant friction between them.

"Wow," Olivia said and started down a hallway. "You never told me that when we talked before."

"It's not something I like to tell a lot of people."

Olivia gave her a sympathetic look. "I understand, but

JANA
DELEON

BAYOU BODYGUARD

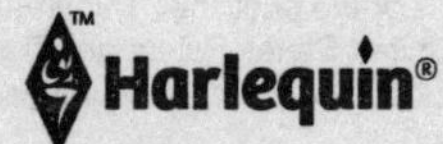

TORONTO NEW YORK LONDON
AMSTERDAM PARIS SYDNEY HAMBURG
STOCKHOLM ATHENS TOKYO MILAN MADRID
PRAGUE WARSAW BUDAPEST AUCKLAND

To my friend, Leigh Zaykoski, for helping me with my new business venture and being a constant source of inspiration.

To my critique partners, Cari Manderscheid and Cindy Taylor, for always helping me improve my work and meet my deadlines. To my friend Colleen Gleason, who talks me off the ledge when I'm frustrated. To my friend Tracey Stanley, for your steadfast support and all your marketing efforts. To my friend Leslie Langtry, it's all good from here on, baby! To my parents, Jimmie and Bobbie Morris, and Jimmie, Donna and Katianne Morris for all your support. To my agent, Kristin Nelson, for being a rock during the turmoil that was 2010. To my editor, Allison Lyons, for giving me the opportunity to write books for the Harlequin line I've always loved to read.

ISBN-13: 978-0-373-69558-4

BAYOU BODYGUARD

This edition published by arrangement with Harlequin Books S.A.

For questions and comments about the quality of this book please contact us at Customer_eCare@Harlequin.ca.

www.Harlequin.com

Printed in U.S.A.

ABOUT THE AUTHOR

Jana DeLeon grew up among the bayous and small towns of southwest Louisiana. She's never actually found a dead body or seen a ghost, but she's still hoping. Jana started writing in 2001 and focuses on murderous plots set deep in the Louisiana bayous. By day, she writes very boring technical manuals for a software company in Dallas. Visit Jana at her website, www.janadeleon.com.

Books by Jana DeLeon

HARLEQUIN INTRIGUE

1265—THE SECRET OF CYPRIERE BAYOU
1291—BAYOU BODYGUARD

CAST OF CHARACTERS

Justine Chatry—The historian jumped at the chance to find the lost emeralds at laMalediction, but her reasons for agreeing to the job weren't purely for business. She hadn't planned on a bodyguard looking over her shoulder as she worked—especially one from her secret past—but was even more unsettled by the way he made her feel.

Brian Marcentel—The former Marine took a leave of absence from the New Orleans Police Department to help out his friend by playing bodyguard. He was expecting trouble, but not from the woman he was hired to protect. His attraction to the beautiful historian wasn't something he planned or welcomed, and when he finally realizes why the Creole beauty looks familiar, it only makes things worse.

Sheriff Blanchard—The good sheriff is suspected of hiding information about the strange occurrences at laMalediction, and is very unhappy to find more people in residence at the estate.

Tom Breaux—The superstitious café owner claims that laMalediction is cursed, but lives in a cabin on the bayou with a path behind it that leads directly to laMalediction. Does he really believe the house is cursed, or does he tell ghost stories to keep others away?

Chris Pauley—The young, brash mechanic has a loud mouth and an abrasive demeanor. He's been caught trespassing at laMalediction, but no one knows what he was doing on the property. What is very clear is that he wants Brian and Justine to leave Cypriere.

Deedee—The café waitress seems easily spooked and refuses to talk about the haunted estate. Justine is certain she's hiding something, but breaking down the scared woman's defenses is going to require finesse and time.

given the situation here, your secondhand knowledge of voodoo may help you with your research."

Justine stared at Olivia. "You don't believe in that stuff, do you?"

"I believe there are more things unexplained than explained here at laMalediction. And I believe the former residents believed in it. Understanding those beliefs may help you find the missing emeralds."

"And fulfill a voodoo prophecy, right?"

Olivia shrugged. "That's what the journals say. I figured a historian like you would love to solve an old mystery with a treasure at the end."

"Yes," Justine agreed, although her reasons for taking the job involved so much more than locating the allegedly cursed emeralds that Olivia referred to. So much more that Justine hadn't told Olivia or anyone else, and didn't intend to. If Olivia knew the real reason Justine had jumped at the chance to access the old journals and photo albums at laMalediction, she may have thought twice about hiring her.

Olivia stepped into a library and set the box she was carrying down on a table in the center of the room. "I figured you'd want to set up shop here in the library. I moved all the books from the underground chamber up here."

Justine looked around the library, at the wall-to-wall bookcases teeming with old books, and could hardly contain her desire to get started. "It's perfect." She pulled a book from one of the shelves and opened it, immediately drawn to the beautiful longhand text inside. "You said you brought everything up from the tunnels? Do you think you and John found everything…all the passageways?"

Olivia frowned. "We hope so. But I don't want to lie to you—we really don't know. I… Damn, there's something

I need to tell you, and I'll understand if you change your mind about staying."

Justine studied Olivia, wondering what had made the calm and collected woman she'd met in New Orleans so nervous. "What's wrong?"

Olivia took a deep breath and blew it out. "When I stayed here before…when all those things happened to me, John and I assumed it was the estate attorney, Ross Wheeler, who was responsible for everything."

Justine nodded. Wheeler had been killed by Olivia's fiancé, John, while holding Olivia hostage in an attempt to force her to reveal the location of the missing emeralds. He'd used the secret passages in the house to spy on her and play tricks with her mind.

"The thing is, the day someone locked me in a tunnel, Wheeler was in court in New Orleans. We just found out a couple of days ago. It couldn't have been him."

Justine took a couple of seconds to process that information. "So someone else was sneaking around besides Wheeler?"

Olivia bit her lower lip. "Yeah, and we don't know who, as there's no indication from Wheeler's documents that he was working with anyone. But the reality is, if that one incident wasn't Wheeler, then some of the others, like the night someone shot at John, may not have been him, either."

"And with Wheeler dead, you can't ask."

"Exactly. John and I talked it over with the new estate attorney and none of us want you or anyone else to be at the house alone. We also don't think it's safe for anyone to stay here at night. You're at a complete disadvantage against anyone who knows the estate, and with the storms that move in, you can become trapped in a matter of minutes. So the estate attorney found a vacant house in town to rent…and John and I sorta convinced the attorney to hire a bodyguard."

"You what?" Surely, she hadn't heard correctly.

"The rental house is right behind Main Street and has two bedrooms. Unfortunately, the owner is out of town until tomorrow, so you can't get the keys until then. The commute isn't bad, as long as it's not raining, and this way you both have a safe place to stay, hopefully where the electricity works better."

Justine frowned. Staying in a rental away from the estate wasn't optimum, but she could hardly blame the estate attorney for being careful. He probably didn't want the liability. Then Olivia's exact wording hit her. "*Both* of us? This bodyguard is staying in the rental house with me?"

"His name is Brian and he's a longtime friend of John's," Olivia rushed to explain. "He's an ex-Marine and works at the New Orleans police department with John. He's overdue for vacation and offered to do this to help us out. I promise you he's completely trustworthy and qualified to protect you. You'll be here at laMalediction during the day and only at the rental at night. Even in closer quarters, I promise Brian won't get in your way."

Despite the ten-thousand-square feet of laMalediction and the unknown amount of acreage to get lost in, the thought of some strange man roaming the halls while she worked bothered Justine on a number of levels. And that was daytime. She couldn't even comprehend staying in close quarters every night with a strange man. Especially a cop. Justine's family didn't have the best of relationships with law enforcement, and she'd grown a bit jaded about the whole "protect and serve" claims they made.

"I don't know…" Justine said, not sure how to argue with what appeared to be a reasonable plan, given the circumstances.

"If you're not comfortable with him, then we'll get someone else. But we can't let you work here alone. I'd feel guilty forever if something happened to you, and, well, the attorney sorta insisted."

Justine sighed. "I understand. It's not that I blame you for being concerned, and I certainly understand the attorney's position. It's just that I have…well, reclusive tendencies."

Olivia placed a hand on her arm and gave her a sympathetic look. "I totally get that, and I'm really sorry that this turned out to be different than what you signed up for. But I hope you'll still take the job. I have a good feeling about you."

Justine smiled. "I'm not going to let a man keep me from this job. It's by far the most intriguing thing I've ever been asked to research. I'm looking forward to it."

The relief on Olivia's face was obvious. "I promise Brian will blend into the background and will not be around unless needed. The attorney scheduled appointments with appraisers and contractors to provide bids for the repairs needed. The old caretaker was only able to minimally maintain the estate, and the house needs a lot of work before it can be sold. Brian will escort those people to do their job while he's here."

The sound of crunching gravel sounded outside the library window and Justine looked out to see a Jeep pull into the courtyard.

"That's him," Olivia said. "I'll go get him so I can introduce you." She hurried out of the room.

Justine stepped up to the window and watched as a hulk of a man stepped out of the Jeep. He was well over six feet tall, and even from a distance, she saw muscles rippling through his T-shirt. His brown hair was cut military short, and his erect stature gave away his Marine background. The intense expression he wore moved swiftly into a smile as Olivia bounced across the driveway to give him a hug.

Justine could tell by the genuineness of the smile and the hug that he liked her, but not in a sexual way. More like a brother-sister sort of thing. His former intensity had made him look dangerous and sexy. The smile made him human. He released Olivia and reached into his Jeep to pull out a duffel bag, and Justine saw a flash of metal at the back of his waistband.

The gun made him a cop.

She stepped back from the window with a sigh. Maybe Brian would be too busy dealing with contractors to get in her way. The thought of a man, much less a cop, watching her every move made the walls seem more narrow, the air in the room thin. She was a woman who needed her space—reveled in it, truth be told.

Olivia stepped into the library, the cop close behind, and waved one hand at Justine as she made the introductions. Justine froze when Olivia said his full name.

"Brian Marcentel."

The blood rushed to her head and she struggled to maintain control. Surely, it couldn't be. She studied his face, hoping it was all a coincidence, but his dark blue eyes gave away the boy she remembered from long ago. Brian extended his hand and Justine hesitated just a moment before placing her hand in his. His hand was solid, with a firm grip, and he studied her as they shook, just like cops always did. Sizing people up.

Did he recognize her? Did he remember? She'd legally changed her name years ago, and the confident woman she was today didn't even remotely resemble the scared child of the past. Was that enough?

Olivia turned to Brian and said, “Justine has reclusive tendencies, so no hovering. Okay?”

A hint of a smile crossed Brian’s face and he held one hand up. “Scout’s honor,” he said to Olivia, then locked his gaze on Justine. “There’s some things I want to go over before we get settled in, about the security and all, but I’ll do my best not to get in your way.”

The light from outside dimmed, as if someone had turned down the power, creating shadows across the library. Olivia looked outside and groaned at the dark clouds swirling above. “My car won’t make it down that path in a rainstorm. I better run.” Olivia looked at Justine, her hesitation and indecision clear as day.

“Go,” Justine reassured her. “Get back home to your fiancé. Brian and I can work out all the details of avoiding each other without a referee.”

Olivia gave her a quick hug, clearly relieved, then grabbed her purse and rushed out of laMalediction without so much as a backward glance. Justine watched her car as it pulled away, the taillights shimmering in the fading light. *She sure didn’t waste any time leaving.*

“So,” she said as she turned to face Brian, “is there a plan? A security system?”

“I’ll start installing the security system tomorrow, here and at the rental, but nothing is in place for tonight. John and I covered every square inch of a couple of bedrooms upstairs and made sure there’s no way in or out except the bedroom door and the windows. We’ll bunk there tonight.”

Justine felt her pulse increase. “Are they next to each other?”

“Yes, and there’s a connecting door. Olivia figures the rooms probably belonged to a child and nanny.”

“Is that really necessary? A connecting door, I mean?”

Justine could already feel the walls closing in on her. The possibility of someone with access to her bedroom, watching her sleep, was far more than she'd bargained for when she'd taken the job.

"John and Olivia think so, and I work for them."

Justine took in the stern expression and the set jaw, and knew it was useless to argue. If Brian was anything like his uncle, he made having things his way a personal crusade. If she wanted to search through the historical documents at laMalediction, she was going to have to find a way to deal with him. "And during the day? Do you plan on sitting across the library table from me as I work?" She couldn't keep the sarcasm from her voice.

Brian narrowed his eyes. "Once the security system is in place, that shouldn't be an issue. I'll carry a remote alarm sensor on me. It will let me know if there's a security breach. I won't be very far away."

"And this security system will be rigged to do what, exactly?"

"Let us know if anyone enters or exits this house or the rental, either through a door or a window."

"So I can't leave either house without setting off an alarm? That's sorta like prison, don't you think?" Justine could feel a flush rising up her neck and she struggled to remain calm. "Look, I know I'm here to do research, but I jog every morning. I spend too much time sitting in a chair to ignore exercising. This job is no different."

Brian nodded. "Give me a time and I'll go with you. I'm used to jogging myself."

Justine bristled. Jogging was her personal time. Granted, she spent most of her time alone, but jogging was when she centered herself for the day ahead and cleansed her mind of everything cluttering it. "I jog alone."

"Not here you don't. This swamp is full of things that can kill you."

"You think I can't handle myself? I grew up in these swamps. I probably know the sounds and tracks of predators better than you."

Brian locked his eyes on hers. "Including human ones?"

Justine stared. "You're serious?"

"Alligators didn't trap Olivia in that tunnel and neither did ghosts. For all we know, Wheeler may not have been behind some of the other things, either. We still haven't figured out how he got to the estate with no one seeing him, and with him dead, there's no way of asking. Could be, whoever else was involved may not be any happier with you here than they were with Olivia."

"Maybe it was kids who locked Olivia in the tunnel." Justine refused to consider the other possibilities.

"You think kids broke into a house that locals fear as haunted to play a practical joke on a stranger?"

"It's not impossible," Justine said, but even as the words left her mouth she knew it wasn't very plausible, either.

"Look," Brian said, "this is the bottom line—John feels something was going on here besides the stuff Wheeler did. I've known John Landry most of my life, and if there's one thing he's got, it's instincts. If he says something's going on here, then there is. And I'm damned well going to find out what it is."

Justine crossed her arms in front of her, a trickle of fear beginning at the back of her mind. "Is that why Olivia was so anxious to leave?"

"Maybe. A lot of bad things happened in this house—to Olivia and to those who lived here before her—and she's seen it all, either in real life or in her dreams. I don't blame her for not wanting to spend another minute here."

Justine stared at him, a bit surprised. "You really believe Olivia saw Marilyn Borque's murder in her dreams? That everything she dreamed was real?"

"Yes, I do."

Justine tried to wrap her mind around such a disciplined personality completely buying into the paranormal. "But if the spirit of Marilyn Borque was trying to get something besides vindication, why did the dreams stop after Wheeler's death?"

"Who says they did?"

Brian grabbed his duffel bag from the floor. "Your room is the second on the left. I'm in the first. We should get settled in before the storm hits and the power goes out." He glanced at the black, swirling sky outside, then left the library.

Who says they did?

Justine felt a chill run through her. She didn't want to believe in the old ways, but what was happening at laMalediction seemed grounded in them. No wonder Olivia wanted to leave. If she was still having the dreams, then whatever malevolent force held laMalediction in its grip wasn't gone.

It was awakened.

Chapter Two

Justine sat her suitcase on the end of the bed, pulled out her nine millimeter and checked the clip. She set the gun on the bed and reached for a pair of yoga pants and a T-shirt. They weren't what she normally slept in, but she wanted to be prepared for anything, including late-night intruders. The last thing she wanted was to chase an intruder through the house, armed with a nine and wearing G-string underwear, like in some cheap B horror movie.

She heard the door close in the next room and glanced over at the adjoining door. Having a cop, especially one from her past, on the other side of that door didn't set well with her, but Olivia had left her no options. Somewhere in the records she was hired to research, she hoped to find the answers she was seeking. Answers that could change her life. For that possibility, she was willing to endure practically anything.

So far, Brian hadn't given any indication that he knew who she was, and with any luck, he wouldn't find out until they were long gone from Cypriere. A knock on the adjoining door brought her out of her thoughts and she shoved her gun back into the suitcase before calling for him to enter. When he stepped into the room, the walls seemed to close in around his large frame. She sucked in a breath. If Brian Marcentel didn't scare an intruder away, she wasn't sure what it would take.

"You okay in here?" Brian asked as he surveyed the room, probably memorizing every square inch.

Justine nodded. "Just getting set up for the ghosts."

Brian stared. "You're doing what?"

Justine pulled a box of salt from her suitcase and began to sprinkle it around items sitting on the dresser. "You put salt around things so that in the morning, you can see if they moved."

"And you think things are going to move on the dresser?"

"I hope not! But if someone is in here besides me or you, I want to know about it."

Brian narrowed his eyes. "So then, how would you know if it was ghosts or people?"

"Doesn't matter to me," Justine replied. "I don't want either of them in my room."

"People are more dangerous."

"That's what I've got *you* for, right?"

"Yeah, but I won't be with you every second. Do you have your nine with you?"

Justine froze and set the salt on the dresser.

"I know you have a nine millimeter registered," Brian continued. "You had to know they'd check you out."

Justine blew out a breath. Of course they would. Olivia had been held hostage by a crazy man and almost killed. They had proof that someone aside from Wheeler was contributing to the problems at laMalediction and Olivia was married to a cop. It would be foolish to think she'd get involved with anyone concerning laMalediction without her fiancé running a thorough background check.

Which meant Brian knew everything about her, too. At least, everything they'd found. How deeply had they looked? Past her name change and into her childhood? Could they even access those records? Olivia hadn't seemed to know anything about her mother when she'd mentioned her earlier. Maybe no one had made the connection to the person she was for the first eighteen years of her life.

"I have my gun," Justine finally replied.

"Do you know how to use it? And I don't mean just the basics."

Justine nodded. "I took lessons at the shooting range, and I practice twice a month. I'm not going to win an Olympic event, but I can take a man down if necessary, and I'm not interested in shooting to injure."

The hint of a smile crossed Brian's face. "I'll make sure I announce myself before entering rooms."

Justine waved a hand in dismissal. "Oh, I promise to look before I shoot—for a second, anyway."

Brian took another look at the salt and frowned. "Well, if you don't need me for anything, I'm going to unload the security equipment from my Jeep before that storms gets going." He pointed to the lantern on the nightstand next to her bed. "I understand the electricity around here is a temporary thing, especially in storms. There are matches in the nightstand drawer for when you need them."

Justine glanced outside at the ever-darkening sky. "Thanks."

Brian gave her a single nod and left the room. Justine watched as he closed the adjoining door then stepped over to the window. The black clouds swirled above the estate like angry pillars of smoke. Justine had seen those clouds often enough to know a heat thunderstorm was on the way and it was going to be a doozy. They were common this time of year, and usually nothing to worry about.

Until now.

Now, she was closed up in a creepy house with a hulking policeman, and in no time she would certainly be without electricity. She watched as Brian pulled a box out of the back of his Jeep, placed it on the front porch then went back for another. Rental houses, security systems, a bodyguard from her past…it was more than she'd bargained for, that was for sure, but then she hadn't expected to feel so edgy, either.

She could blame the feeling on sharing close quarters with a cop, or on the fear that he'd remember her, but that wouldn't be completely true. One thing Justine never did was lie to herself. Like it or not, her uneasiness came from knowing that Wheeler hadn't been the lone gunman. That someone else had access to laMalediction and could still enter undetected.

And more importantly, that Olivia's dreams continued.

She heard a creaking sound outside the bedroom door and stiffened. A single glance out the window confirmed that Brian was still unloading boxes. It could just be the house settling, but every instinct inside her screamed that it wasn't. Silently, she eased her gun from the suitcase and crept to the door.

She peered into the hallway, but it was empty. Then at the end of the hallway, a shadow slid out of an open doorway. Tightening her grip on her pistol, she slipped into the hallway and inched toward the doorway. The shadow lengthened for a second, then disappeared back into the room. All thoughts of safety aside, she sprinted down the hallway and burst into the room, but there was no one in sight.

She took a deep breath and let it out slowly, trying to calm her racing heart. A quick survey of the room told her nothing. A couple of cardboard boxes and a small table lined the far wall, but otherwise, the room was empty. She crossed the room and took a closer look at the boxes, even shifted the top one of the stack, but all she found was a thick layer of dust that caused her to sneeze.

She slowly walked around the room, feeling the walls, looking for an entry point, but the plastered walls looked seamless in every aspect. The single window in the room was closed and locked, and when she attempted to open it, it held fast, glued into place by ancient paint. Frustrated, she blew out a breath. Building construction and hidden passageways were not her forte. Justine had never set foot in a place so grand that it housed servants, much less provided them hidden passageways to conduct their daily work while remaining invisible to visitors. Still, for someone to have disappeared so quickly, shouldn't she see a sign somewhere?

She walked back to her bedroom, trying to put this latest occurrence into perspective. Maybe something blowing in the wind had passed the window in the room, casting a shadow into the hall. Okay, so the window was at the completely wrong angle and there hadn't been even a breath of wind when she looked outside, but wasn't that just as plausible as a disappearing person, or even worse, a ghost?

Or maybe her overactive imagination played a trick on her. She wasn't given to fancy, but it wasn't impossible. A lot was riding on her work at laMalediction. That, coupled with Olivia's unnerving behavior earlier and the unwanted introduction from her past, was certainly enough to put her on edge.

She crossed her bedroom and looked out the window in time to see Brian locking his Jeep. He didn't look even remotely disturbed or alerted to anything out of order. Sighing, she slipped her gun back into her suitcase, disgusted that she'd allowed herself to be so easily spooked.

And that's when she noticed the piece of folded paper on the nightstand.

Her breath caught in her throat. That paper hadn't been there before, but now it sat perched on the thin layer of salt she'd poured earlier. She knew she shouldn't touch it. She should call for Brian. Let him do his cop thing with fingerprints and such, but she couldn't stop herself from reaching for it, opening it.

She gasped as she looked at it. Tears stung her eyes at the picture of her mother, secured in a straitjacket, locked behind bars, her face still fresh with bruises from the "helpful" law-enforcement officers who had dragged her away.

"I know who you are."

The words were written just above the photo.

She crumpled the paper and tucked it in her pocket. She'd burn it at the first opportunity.

But no matter what, she wouldn't be scared away from laMalediction. Whoever had left the paper was brazen, especially with the cop right outside, and that told her one of two things: he was either crazy or desperate.

Either could work in her favor.

BRIAN TOSSED HIS GUN and keys onto the bedroom dresser, then stepped into the tiny bathroom to turn on the water in the bath, wishing like hell someone had thought to update the antiquated bathrooms in the main house to include showers. Taking baths in a relic of a house in the middle of nowhere and babysitting angry women with a fear of cops—he'd reached an all-time low. Granted, this job gave him the opportunity to take a much-needed break from police work, and for that he was grateful, but it came with other complications that he was usually able to avoid.

Like angry, beautiful women with a fear of cops.

He tensed for a moment and rubbed the two-day growth on his jaw. Where had that beautiful part come from? Granted, when Olivia had told him she'd hired a historian, he'd been expecting the gray-haired-librarian sort. A dark-skinned Creole beauty with green eyes, miles of black, wavy hair and a body that was toned to perfection had never entered his mind. Not to mention there was something familiar about her. Something he couldn't quite put his finger on, but it would come to him eventually.

He stepped back into the bedroom and grabbed some clean clothes from his duffel bag just as a huge bolt of lightning struck outside. The lights flickered twice, then went out completely, leaving him in total darkness. He took a couple of steps to his right, trying to feel for the lantern in the inky, black room, and banged his knee on the nightstand. Mentally cursing himself for doing the very thing he'd warned Justine to be prepared for, he located the matches and lit the lantern.

He placed the lantern on the center of the nightstand and tossed his clean clothes on the bed. It was probably a bad idea to submerge yourself in a tub of water during a thunderstorm. Pulling the heavy drapes to the side, he peered outside at the rain that poured from the sky. These blinding-heat thunderstorms that blew in off the Gulf of Mexico were nothing new to him, but while normally he could ignore the storm and go to bed, being at laMalediction spurred his thoughts to all the things a storm this bad implied.

Communication would be nonexistent, and if there was an emergency, he wasn't certain they'd be able to make it down the path to Cypriere, even in his Jeep. It was also far easier for someone to hide in a blinding rainstorm, both their movements and the noise they made, so he needed to be more alert than ever.

Brian released the drapes, but as the heavy curtain slipped back into place, he saw a flash of white across the courtyard. He yanked the drape back again and focused on the area behind the fountain where he'd seen the white object, but there was nothing there.

He waited a couple of seconds and was just about to chalk it up to debris blowing in the storm when he saw it again, this time clearer. It was a tall figure wearing a long, white robe. He couldn't see a face, but he had no doubt the object was human. The person stood just at the edge of the woods, motionless in the storm as the white robe whipped around him.

Brian dropped the drape and reached for his gun. No way was someone standing out in that rainstorm to bring a housewarming gift. After his conversations with John and Olivia, he'd anticipated trouble, but not necessarily so soon. He shoved his gun into the waistband of his jeans, grabbed a flashlight and knocked once on the connecting door before entering Justine's room. She sat in a chair at a writing table and stiffened as he entered the room, her expression both aggravated and indignant.

"That wasn't much notice," she complained. "What if I'd been dressing?"

"There's someone outside in the storm, standing across the courtyard. I'm going to check it out. I need you to lock both doors to your room and do not come out until I tell you it's clear."

Justine's eyes widened and she glanced out the window into the storm. "Someone's out there in that? But that's crazy!"

"Exactly my point," he said as he opened the door to

her room and slipped into the hallway. "Stay put until I get back." He pulled the door closed and rushed out of the house and into the storm.

Chapter Three

Justine rushed to lock doors as soon as Brian left, then pulled her gun from her suitcase and checked the clip. Placing the gun within easy reach on the writing table, she took a breath and tried to process what Brian had told her. It was so unbelievable, she was still having trouble wrapping her mind around it.

She knew that standing in front of the window during a lightning storm was a dangerous thing to do. Not only because of the lightning, but because she'd left the drapes open earlier to watch the storm, and the lantern would cast her silhouette onto the window. Even the most amateur of shooters would find that an easy target.

Not that she had any reason to believe that someone was trying to kill her, but she had every reason to believe that someone was trying to scare her. A well-placed shot through a window would be a good way to scare someone, but could also result in disaster with the high winds of the storm. Edging across the room, she stopped just before the window and leaned over to peer outside.

The storm was raging and she had to strain to make out Brian as he slipped behind the automobiles in the courtyard. After that, the fountain came into clearer view and she got her visual bearings. Scanning the courtyard, she looked for anything out of place…like someone standing in the middle of a torrential downpour just asking to be struck by lightning.

Across the courtyard, just beyond the woods, she saw what had sent Brian running outside. She dimmed the lamp to barely an ember to remove the glare from the window, and looked outside again. The figure was still there, wearing a white-hooded cape that whipped around in the storm. She strained to make out a face or even to tell if the figure was a man or a woman, but the head was bent, as if staring at the ground.

Suddenly the figure raised his head, and Justine would have sworn on everything holy that whatever was out in the storm was looking directly at her. Two red eyes glowed inside the white hood and her heart began to race. Her skin tingled and her hair stood on end as a wave of fear like she'd never experienced before washed over her.

She drew back from the window, her body flat against the wall, and struggled to breathe normally, her heart pounding so loudly she thought it would burst. What in God's name was out there? And where was Brian? She hadn't seen him at all. Had that…that *thing* gotten him?

You're panicking. Get a grip. It has to be a trick.

She sucked in a deep breath and slowly blew it out, then leaned over and peeked outside again. But this time the courtyard was empty. No white-hooded figure. No red eyes.

No Brian.

She scanned beyond the courtyard, past the caretaker's cottage and the storage shed and into the woods. Surely Brian wouldn't have gone into the woods. He was armed, but if someone was playing a trick on them, they were obviously prepared, and Justine had to assume, better equipped to disappear, even in the storm. What Justine had seen required planning and setup and careful deliberation.

Certainly not the sort of thing kids would pull off, as the sheriff had suggested to Olivia.

She scanned the courtyard once more, looking for any sign of Brian, and her hands clenched involuntarily as every square inch she could see turned up empty. How long did she wait? Hours? All night? What if he needed help?

Justine was an excellent tracker, but in a storm like this, even she would have trouble determining whether the telltale signs of a presence in the woods were due to a man passing or the winds and rain of the storm. Footprints wouldn't remain for long in the downpour.

Frustrated and antsy, she blew out a breath and paced the length of the room. On the second pass, her nose wrinkled and she stopped to sniff the air. Something was different…acrid.

Smoke!

Blood rushed to her head and she clutched the desk to remain steady. The room went out of focus for a moment, then seemed to tilt. She closed her eyes and concentrated on breathing, on regaining control.

Think.

But there was little to think about. There was only one way out of the second floor that she knew of, and that was down the main stairwell. She shoved her keys into her pocket then lifted her pistol from the desktop and crossed the room to the door. She ran her hand across the surface of the bedroom door to check for heat, but felt none.

This is it.

She stared at the dead bolt and took a deep breath. Finally, she slid it back and eased the bedroom door open to peer into the hallway. The smell of smoke was much stronger in the hallway, but she couldn't see smoke or hear any sign of fire. More importantly, she didn't see anyone with red eyes wearing a white robe.

Her best option was to get out of the house, even if the road to Cypriere was unpassable. The house was old and huge and the fire could be anywhere below or above her. Either could create a collapse, so her car was the safest place to be, assuming there was nothing in the courtyard that was more dangerous than fire.

Not allowing her mind to dwell on that possibility, she hurried down the hall toward the stairwell and rushed downstairs to the entry. Stopping short at the front door, she peered out the narrow side windows to ensure the courtyard was clear. As she reached for the doorknob, she heard something behind her, but before she could turn around and take aim, something hard struck the back of her head and she dropped to the floor, everything fading to black.

THE RAIN CAME DOWN in blinding sheets and soaked Brian completely before he'd even made it twenty feet from the house. He wiped the excess moisture away from his eyes, wishing he'd thought to grab his ball cap on the way out. He skirted around the edge of the courtyard, moving from one hiding place to another without using the flashlight, trying to limit his exposure. When he'd made it completely across the courtyard, he hid behind the storage shed near the caretaker's cottage and then slipped into the edge of the woods just beyond.

He looked back at the house to get his bearings, and saw the dull glow of the lantern light cast from the windows of the bedrooms that he and Justine occupied. He looked across the courtyard from the windows and estimated the location where he'd seen the figure. The area was empty now, but if someone had been standing out in this storm, they would have left footprints in the thick, gummy Louisiana mud, even in the downpour.

He moved steadily through the edge of the woods toward the spot where he'd seen the figure, then scanned the courtyard and the woods beyond for any sign of movement. Nothing. He waited a couple of seconds, but nothing moved except the storm.

Finally, he left his hiding place in the woods and walked to the ground where he'd seen the person standing. He turned on the flashlight and shined it on the ground.

No way.

He shined the light back and forth across the muddy ground, looking for the trail that had to be there—the trail that should indicate how the person arrived or where they'd gone. But the ground held no prints at all. He turned around and shined the light across the ground where he'd walked and saw the outline of his footprints in the mud.

Even with the intensity of the rain, there wasn't enough time for footprints to have washed away—not in a matter of minutes. He walked to the edge of the woods and shined the flashlight along the perimeter, looking for any sign that someone had entered or exited the courtyard through the woods.

His frustration grew with every step he took. He hadn't imagined the figure, and he knew he was looking in the right area. But no one could have walked across that ground without leaving a trace.

No one but a ghost.

And that just wasn't possible. He'd never believed in that sort of thing before, and regardless of what Olivia thought she'd seen when Wheeler held her captive, and the huge amount of respect he had for her, he wasn't about to start buying in to it now. There was a logical explanation for everything happening at laMalediction.

And he was going to get to the bottom of it.

He entered the woods just behind the area where he'd seen the figure and scanned the ground for any sign of passage. There was some broken foliage along the edge of the woods, but the force of the storm could have caused that as easily as a man. What a storm couldn't do was leave footprints and there had to be footprints somewhere.

He covered at least a hundred-foot stretch of woods, ten feet deep into the brush, but turned up nothing. Glancing at his watch, he realized he'd been gone from the house for over thirty minutes. He didn't like the idea of leaving Justine in there alone, especially not at night and during a storm.

He glanced back at the house and his heart began to beat faster. The light from Justine's room barely showed through the window, when earlier it had been bright. Abandoning his investigation, he ran straight across the courtyard to the house, his mind racing with a multitude of possibilities, none of them good.

No way had she turned off the lamp and gone to bed and he'd made sure it was full of oil when he checked on her earlier. If she was afraid of someone seeing her, she could have drawn the drapes, but he could still make out the dark lines of the heavy fabric drawn to the sides of the window.

He burst through the front door, prepared to dash upstairs, but his foot connected with a solid object in the dark and sent him sprawling across the marble floor of the entry. He directed his flashlight to the floor and a single glance back confirmed his worst fear. He scrambled over to Justine, who lay across the entry.

Leaning in, he watched her chest and saw it rise and fall. A quick check of her pulse showed a somewhat elevated heartbeat, but nothing alarming. "Justine," he said and patted the sides of her cheeks, trying to wake her. "Justine."

His pulse quickened as he failed to get any response. He slipped his arms underneath her and carried her into the sitting room where he placed her on the couch. A lantern sat on a table next to the couch, so he lit it to cast more light on the situation. As he placed the lantern on the coffee table closer to Justine, she stirred.

And that's when he saw blood on the couch pillow.

He froze for a moment, then knelt down and gently lifted her head, trying to see what was causing the bleeding. The gash was immediately visible, and he let out a sigh of relief as he realized that the cut wasn't deep or large, and was probably made by something with a fairly sharp end, rather than the marble floor, as he'd originally feared. She must have slipped and hit her head on something. But what?

There was nothing in the center of the entry where he'd found her, so the only other logical explanation was that she'd hit it somewhere close by and staggered to the center of the entry where she'd passed out. He stepped through the other side of the sitting room and into the kitchen. He'd noticed clean dishtowels in a drawer earlier, so he grabbed one and soaked it with cold water. Justine still hadn't wakened when he returned to the sitting room, so he placed the cool cloth across her forehead.

She stirred a bit and her eyes fluttered. Then all of a sudden, she sat bolt upright, her eyes wide with fright. He grabbed her arms as she tried to strike him.

"Justine, it's Brian. You're safe. Stop struggling or you may injure yourself."

Justine locked her gaze on him and he could see the panic in her eyes begin to diminish. She gasped for air, then blew out a huge breath and swung her legs around so she was in a sitting position.

"What happened?" she asked.

Brian shook his head. "I found you passed out on the entry floor. You've got a gash on the back of your head. I figure maybe you fell in the dark and hit your head on something."

Now that the initial crisis had passed, Brian felt irritation begin. "Things like this are exactly why I told you to stay put. You can't just walk around in the pitch-black in a strange house. You're going to be lucky if you don't need stitches."

"There was a fire," Justine argued. "I smelled the smoke in my room, and stronger in the hallway."

Brian frowned. "I don't smell anything, and if there was a fire we'd see it by now. Are you sure?"

"Of course I'm sure. Do you think I would risk leaving the room with that…that thing outside if I didn't have a good reason? I know you're here to protect me, but I didn't exactly grow up in Mayberry. Survival is something I'm very familiar with."

Brian sat on the coffee table and sighed. "So what happened after you left the room?"

Justine stared at the wall behind him, her brow scrunched in concentration. "I figured the safest place to go was my car. I checked the bedroom door before opening it. It was cool, but the smell of smoke was stronger in the hall. I hurried downstairs and looked out the entry window to make sure the outside was clear."

She frowned and Brian could see she was struggling to remember.

"Did you see something outside?" he prompted.

"No…I heard something…inside." Her eyes widened. "Directly behind me in the entry, but before I could turn around, something hit me on the back of the head and everything went black."

"Damn it!" Brian jumped up from the coffee table and paced the room. "I should have known better. Stupid, stupid, stupid."

"What should you have known? I don't understand."

"It was all a trick to get to you. The person outside to draw me out of the house. The smell of smoke to get you out of the locked room. All so someone could take a shot at you."

Justine sucked in a breath. "But that's crazy. Why would someone go to all that trouble just to hit me? If they'd wanted me dead, I would be."

Brian frowned at Justine's words because he knew she was right. There had been plenty of time to kill her if that was the intent. "Maybe someone wants to scare you away."

"But why me? Why not go after you? You're the strongest."

Brian shook his head. "All I can figure is that someone is unhappy about your work here."

"How would anyone even know about it?"

"It's a small place. I'm sure word has already gotten around about most everything that's happened here. A lot of the story was splashed all over the New Orleans newspapers, and the Cypriere locals probably all know what really went down. All anyone would have to do is figure out what you do for a living and they could put two and two together."

"I thought the missing emeralds were a secret, assuming they're even still around. The only other thing I'm here to do is research the Borque ancestry. Why would anyone care about that?"

"No one should care, and that's exactly what I don't like

about all this. Olivia and John didn't make the emeralds public knowledge because they didn't want the estate besieged by treasure hunters."

"That makes sense. And the locals have probably passed down tales of the emeralds and other things at laMalediction for generations. A local would have looked for them before now if he thought they really existed."

"Maybe he has been looking and wasn't successful. News of the hidden journals was made public. Maybe he thinks the journals will lead you right to the very thing he's been looking for."

"This is so convoluted."

Brian nodded. "John and Olivia anticipated trouble when they asked me to come here, but I know for a fact, they didn't expect anything like this." He placed a hand on Justine's arm. "I think you ought to consider leaving. Pack up the journals and albums and take them back with you to New Orleans."

"No way. The emeralds are not hidden in any of those books, and that's what Olivia's paying me to do. If they even exist and can be found, they're going to be at laMalediction."

Brian blew out a breath. She was right but he didn't have to like it. "Okay, then we stay, but we're going to have to come up with a strategy. Someone prepared for us, so right now he has the advantage. We have to make sure we do everything to level the playing field. That means, if you want to stay, you do everything I ask with no argument. Got it?"

The apprehensive and somewhat belligerent expression on Justine's face gave away her real feelings, but she nodded.

For now, he guessed that would have to do.

Chapter Four

Justine awakened before dawn the next morning, but that was no surprise. She'd never been a heavy sleeper, and the previous night hadn't been exactly restful. She sat up in bed and gingerly felt the back of her head. The lump was still there, but had decreased significantly in size. It was tender to the touch, but her headache was gone, so she figured the worst of it was over. She threw back the covers and eased out of bed, careful not to jar her head and start the throbbing all over again.

The connecting door to Brian's room was partway open, so she eased over to it and peeked inside. Brian was sprawled on top of the bed, covers bunched in a ball at the foot of the bed. He wore only a T-shirt and drawstring shorts, and Justine couldn't help but admire the toned, tanned length of his muscular arms and legs. As much as being closed up with a man, especially this man, made her uneasy, she had to admit that, as far as bodyguards went, Brian appeared to be a competent one. Certainly his bravery wasn't in question, given what he'd chased in the courtyard the night before.

She pulled the connecting door almost shut, hoping the sound of her moving around wouldn't wake him. He'd tended to her head last night in a gentle way that she'd found surprising, then he'd insisted on helping her to bed and to two shots of whiskey. He'd sat in the rocking chair in the corner and claimed he wasn't leaving until she fell asleep. Justine had no idea what time he left her room, but figured he could probably use the rest.

She eased out of the bedroom and down the stairs to the kitchen. Coffee and aspirin were her first orders of business. She couldn't afford a headache, with everything she needed to do today, any more than she could afford to be unfocused. Between the caffeine and the aspirin, she should be ready to take on the world—or at least her research. Olivia had indicated she'd left supplies in the kitchen and Justine sighed with relief when she pulled out a sealed package of gourmet coffee.

Pulling the package apart, Justine took in the rich smell of the grounds and gave Olivia a mental blessing. Her employer had seriously good taste in coffee. She filled the coffeepot, figuring Brian wouldn't be able to pass up a cup, once the smell had permeated the entire downstairs, and while the coffee brewed, she checked out the refrigerator and pantry. Olivia had understated the amount of food she'd provided. Both the pantry and refrigerator were full of tasty and easy-to-prepare items.

Justine pulled a strawberry breakfast bar out of the pantry and waited impatiently for the coffee to finish brewing. She'd just taken her first heavenly sip when Brian entered the kitchen.

"Man, that smells fantastic," Brian said, and took in a deep whiff of the coffee.

"It *is* fantastic," Justine said as she removed a coffee mug from the cabinet and handed it to Brian. "If Olivia was here, I'd kiss her."

Brian poured a steamy cup of coffee and smiled. "I didn't know you swung that way."

Justine smiled at his teasing. "For this coffee, I may consider it."

"I'll keep that in mind in case I want something," he said as he took a seat at the kitchen table. He took a drink of the coffee and sighed. "You're right. If John wouldn't shoot me, I'd kiss Olivia, too."

Justine laughed, then caught herself and opened the pantry door again, pretending to inspect the contents. It unnerved her how easily she'd slipped into a comfort level with Brian. She always had her guard up, for good reason, and now, despite the best reasons of all, this man was able to get her guard down. She wasn't even going to assess the reason why, as that might lead to all sorts of questions she didn't want to address. Not now, nor anytime in the future.

She felt his eyes on her and looked over at him. Despite the stellar coffee he frowned, and Justine steeled herself, knowing that whatever he was thinking was probably something she wasn't going to like.

"How's your head?" he asked.

"It's fine. A little tender still, but my headache was gone when I woke up. It aches a little now, since I've been moving around, but nothing unexpected given the circumstances."

"I think we should call the sheriff," he said. "You could have been seriously injured or even killed when you fell last night. The fact that someone attacked you the first night here doesn't sit well with me at all, but ultimately it's the sheriff's responsibility."

Justine closed the pantry door. "You really think he's going to do anything about it? He wasn't exactly a big help for Olivia, from what I heard."

"No, he wasn't. And no, I don't really think he'll do much of anything. Quite frankly, I don't know that he's got the skills to, but what I do think he'll do is spread the word around that you have a bodyguard and I'm not afraid to fire a weapon. It shouldn't take long for that bit of gossip to spread through Cypriere. Maybe someone will think twice about that stunt last night when they realize how deadly the outcome could be."

His words made sense, but the last thing Justine wanted to do was deal with more cops. More people who might dig into her past. "Whatever you think," she said finally, knowing that he was going to do it whether she agreed with him or not. Putting up an argument would only make him suspicious when notifying the cops was the normal thing to do.

"Let me know when he's here," she said. "I'm going to start setting up in the library." She refilled her cup of coffee and left the kitchen before Brian could clue in on her sudden case of nerves.

DESPITE THE THIRTY-MINUTE reprieve she had while setting up in the library, Justine felt a lump in her throat when Brian called to her from the front entry that the sheriff had arrived.

He's just going to ask some questions. Olivia told you he was useless. He's nothing to fear.

If she kept telling herself that, maybe she'd start to believe it.

She walked down the hall into the entry, assessing Sheriff Blanchard as she shook his hand. He was older, probably late fifties, if his silver-and-black hair was any indication. His expression was one of clear annoyance, even though he politely shook her hand and addressed her as "ma'am."

Brian directed them to the kitchen, and Justine took a

seat across the table from the sheriff while Brian leaned against the kitchen counter to her left.

Sheriff Blanchard studied her for a moment and she struggled not to look away. Finally, he spoke. "Mr. Marcentel says you had a bit of trouble here last night. You want to tell me about it?"

Justine looked over at Brian and he started telling the sheriff about the figure standing in the courtyard.

"Standing in the middle of the storm wearing a dress?" Sheriff Blanchard stared at Brian as if he'd lost his mind. "Someone would have to be crazy and have a death wish. Besides, how did they get here and where did they disappear to afterward? You said yourself there were no tracks."

Justine saw Brian's jaw flex and knew he was getting angry. "Are you saying I imagined what I saw?"

Sheriff Blanchard shrugged. "Wouldn't be the first time people saw stuff that wasn't there. This house has a history that can play with the mind. All I'm suggesting is that, maybe with everything that happened to your friend before, you're looking for something to be wrong now."

Brian straightened up, but before he could respond, Justine said, "So, did we *share* a delusional vision, Sheriff? Because I saw the same thing that Brian did. I might agree with a diagnosis of collective insanity if Brian and I shared a close past raised by people rooted in those beliefs. But considering I just met him yesterday, I seriously doubt we formed that sort of bond while unpacking."

"Now don't get your back up," Sheriff Blanchard said. "I wasn't trying to suggest—"

"Yes, you were," Justine said, "and you're wrong. Tell me, Sheriff, if that figure outside was just our imagination, then who hit me on the back of the head? I'm not imagining the gash or the headache, and I fell in the middle of the entryway where there is nothing for me to strike my head on."

Sheriff Blanchard sighed. "What would you like me to tell you? That you hit your head somewhere else and wandered into the entry before you collapsed? That you and your friend here spooked yourselves and imagined it all? I don't have any other answers. Until Olivia Markham came to this house, hadn't nothing untoward happened here for a hundred years. Maybe that should tell you all something."

Justine felt heat rise to her face as the sheriff talked, and she was ready to attack when she felt Brian's hand squeeze her shoulder. She looked up at the former Marine, who gave her an imperceptible "no."

"I understand your position," Brian said to the sheriff. "Cypriere being such a close-knit town and us being outsiders, you don't want to get involved. I'll be happy to call the state police to look at the situation. That should relieve you of the duty of investigating your friends and family, which would probably be a conflict of interest, anyway."

Sheriff Blanchard rose from the table and glared at Brian. "Are you saying I'm not capable of doing my job?"

"No. I'm saying it's inconvenient for you to do your job."

"Fine," Sheriff Blanchard said, his jaw clenched. "You want me to see if some kids are pulling pranks on you, I will. You want me to figure out how she got that knot on her head, I'll need to go over this entire house to find what made that cut. But as my only deputy is on his honeymoon, I can't manage that sort of investigation for a couple of days. I still have a town to protect."

Sheriff Blanchard shot one final look of disdain at Justine and Brian, then spun around and left the house. As the door closed behind him, Justine realized Brian's hand was still on her shoulder. Suddenly the room was too small or he was too close, or both. Before she could move, he dropped his hand and stepped away from the table.

"I don't think he's going to be much help," Brian said.

"Doesn't look like it. What do you think the problem is?"

Brian shrugged. "No telling, really, but my guess is he's probably getting ready to retire and doesn't want this mess interfering with his coasting along to those pension checks. He's probably turned a blind eye to things happening out here for years, dismissing it as kids or thrill seekers."

"He doesn't believe us."

"No."

"Why didn't you tell him you were a cop? Don't you guys have some kind of unspoken code where you have to believe each other?"

"I don't trust the man. Maybe he's just incompetent and lazy, but either way, I'm not offering up any information. If he wants to know anything about us, he's going to have to ask or run a background check." Brian grabbed a bottled water from the refrigerator. "I'm going to start installing the security system. If you need me, I'll be within yelling distance."

Justine watched as he exited the kitchen through the sitting room. He was clearly aggravated with the sheriff's attitude, but he hadn't pushed the issue. In fact, he'd prevented her from causing a scene, and for that she was glad. The last thing she needed was the sheriff digging into her past and determining he had a good reason to accuse her of imagining things, but the way Brian had left things, that may be exactly what the sheriff did.

Instantly, her mind flashed back to the photo of her mother and the message she'd found in her room the day before. Someone in Cypriere already knew who she was or someone had followed her to Cypriere. But who? And why?

Justine touched her shoulder where Brian's hand had rested. It was almost as if he'd sensed her discomfort as soon as she felt it and stepped away from her. Was he really that intuitive?

If so, Justine had to be very, very careful around Brian Marcentel.

JUSTINE PLACED the two stacks of journals on the table in the library and plugged in her laptop, ready to get to work. She'd organized by date the journals written by Marilyn Borque, the murdered mistress of laMalediction, and the journals written by her personal maid, Sissy Dubois. She hoped that by reading them together, she could form a clear vision of the events during that time.

Olivia had already filled her in on Marilyn Borque's background. The poor woman had essentially been sold to Franklin Borque just before the Civil War by her father to seal a business deal. Franklin built the monstrosity, laMalediction, when no town existed within a hundred miles, effectively cutting his young wife off from civilization. The remote location made it easy for him to beat her without coming under question.

Franklin left for the war the following year and Marilyn sent for her lover. When Franklin returned, he was more crazed than before and had obtained a lion statue with giant emeralds for eyes. Marilyn was certain the acquisition was not legal, but Franklin's obsession with the statue was a far bigger concern. Sissy sent Marilyn to her cousin, a voodoo priestess, for help and the two formed a plan to contain the evil that rested in the emerald eyes of the statue. When Franklin discovered that his prize possession was missing, he murdered Marilyn and was then struck by lightning the same night in the middle of the courtyard.

Justine opened a marked spot in one of the diaries to reread the entry Olivia had flagged.

June 15, 1863
I took the statue to Sissy's cousin tonight. She had a violent reaction to the piece as soon as she saw the eyes. The emeralds, she said, are cursed. She removed the emeralds from the statue and placed them in a pouch for safekeeping, then performed a spell on the statue to separate it from the evil in the stones. We then broke the statue and crushed the pieces until they were dust. We collected the dust in a jar and will fling it far into the bayou, where the spirits that inhabit the water can prevent it from resurfacing. She will bind the emeralds in metal and cast a spell two nights from now when the moon is full. Then I will hide them in a safe place.

I know this is the only way, but I feel overwhelming guilt for the future I am creating for my descendants. The stones will not remain bound forever. One day, the emeralds will call on those of my lineage to fulfill the prophecy that I have set in motion.

Even if it costs their lives.

Justine set the journal to the side and opened a document file on her laptop. She began to make notes on possible avenues for research. Sissy's cousin had lived in a Creole village with other descendants from Haiti who still practiced the old ways. Memories from her childhood gave Justine an understanding of the purpose behind binding an object in another the way the woman had bound the emeralds in metal to cut off the energy that emitted from them. But Sissy's cousin would have insisted on a double binding if she thought the emeralds were cursed—the first binding by man, the second by nature.

Justine blew out a breath and leaned back in the chair. Olivia had been right. Her knowledge of the old ways would give her an edge, as much as she was loath to admit it. The most logical way to bind the stones with nature would be to bury them, but where? Certainly, Sissy's cousin would have insisted the stones remain on the estate, as it was the family's responsibility to watch over the evil they'd brought to this place. But the estate consisted of not only laMalediction but hundreds of acres of swamp.

There had to be a clue in the journals about where Marilyn had hidden the emeralds. That was the angle she'd start working on first. With any luck, her research of the journals would provide her the answers she was looking for in her personal quest—the real reason she'd taken the job. Even if the journals yielded nothing, she was still convinced the answers she sought lay somewhere in laMalediction. And she was going to find them.

"How's it going?" Brian's voice broke into her thoughts, causing her to jump.

"Sorry," he said as he stepped into the library. "I didn't mean to startle you."

"It's not your fault. When I'm lost in the work, I tend to filter out everything around me." She gave him a rueful look. "Probably not the best trait, given the situation here, right?"

Brian shrugged. "You're a researcher. If you couldn't focus on your research to the exclusion of everything else, you probably wouldn't be very good at your job. Let me worry about catching the bad guys—that's what *I* do naturally."

Justine leaned back in her chair, considering Brian's words. "So you think the man upstairs had a master plan for all of us, and doled out talent accordingly? Then where do people like Franklin Borque fit into your theory? I assume you know the history."

Brian nodded. "Olivia told me what she found. I don't know what makes people like Franklin Borque, but I do believe I've stared evil in the face in Iraq."

Justine sat upright in her chair. "What does it look like? Evil?"

"Sometimes beautiful and seductive, sometimes so normal that it never registers on your radar…until it's too late." He stared out the library window for a moment, then looked back at Justine. "But there's always those moments…and if you're paying attention, you can catch one of them. When the facade relaxes and just for an instant, you see it in their eyes. Then in a flash, it's gone, leaving you wondering if you ever saw it in the first place."

Justine crossed her arms across her chest, a sudden chill running through her body. "Do you still wonder when you see it now?"

"Not anymore. I would recognize it now." He paused. "It's funny, you know. Good can take on many appearances, many faces, but evil always looks the same.

"Anyway," he said, "I came to tell you there's a storm brewing. It's almost three, so I figure we may as well head into town and get everything settled with the rental house. I've got to load a couple of boxes in my Jeep, so just meet me out front when you've wrapped up in here."

Justine stared out the library window, watching Brian

as he rolled up the soft top on the back of his Jeep. What kind of horrors had Brian Marcentel seen? And more importantly, would he see them again in Cypriere?

Chapter Five

Justine waited in front of laMalediction as Brian loaded the last box. He couldn't help but notice how striking she was as she stood in front of the stained-glass windows, her long hair rippling in the breeze. She looked as if she fit here. He'd thought the same thing when he saw her deep in thought in the library. He'd like to think it was because the house was deep in a swamp and Justine was Creole, but there was something more to it than that. Something that he couldn't quite place, and that bothered him.

"I put my suitcase in my car, but I can move it if I'm riding with you," Justine said, breaking him out of his thoughts.

"I figured you could follow me in your car. The road should have dried from the rain yesterday. We have a better chance of getting in and out of here every day using my Jeep, so I figured we'd leave your car at the rental house, assuming you don't have any objection. I'm not convinced it would be safe here at night."

"No. That sounds perfectly reasonable." Justine pulled her keys from her backpack and hopped in her car.

Brian climbed in his Jeep and waited until Justine gave him a wave before pulling away from laMalediction. He checked his rearview mirror to make sure Justine was behind him, then continued at a slow pace down the rough dirt path that led to Cypriere. In his mirrors, he could see laMalediction fading into the swamp, and with every foot he put between himself and the house, it was as if a weight lifted from him.

Surprised, he mulled that bit of revelation over in his mind. He hadn't realized that being in the house cast that much of a shadow over him, and it was something he needed to carefully monitor. It was easy to take on the emotional energy of a place and the people. He'd learned that in Iraq. That level of intuition had saved his life on more than one occasion, but on the flip side, if he allowed himself to become mired in the energy surrounding him, it took the edge off his response time and dulled his critical thinking.

Feel, then analyze.

Apparently, his mind had decided he'd entered hostile territory, so he needed to keep his mantra in mind. Odd, that his ability had never once surfaced while working as a cop, but it had come back full force when he arrived at laMalediction. Odd *and* disconcerting.

He cut off his train of thought as he drove into Cypriere. The owner of the rental house promised to leave the keys with the café owner, Tom, so Brian pulled into a parking space in front of the café. Justine pulled in next to him.

"We're supposed to pick up the keys at the café," he explained to Justine as she joined him on the sidewalk in front of the place. "If you're hungry, I figured we could eat supper here. We'll need to stock the rental house, and quite frankly, I don't feel like grocery shopping at the moment."

She hesitated for just a second then nodded. "Fine by me. I totally skipped lunch."

Brian opened the door and waited while she stepped into the café, wondering if during her hesitation she'd decided that eating with him in a public place was preferable to eating with him alone in the rental house. He'd been warned that she was reclusive, but from what he observed, Justine acted guarded.

It took him a minute to realize that she wasn't moving forward. One look around the café filled him in on the why. Every patron in the place sat frozen in time. Even the waitress had stopped serving to stare at them. Feeling as if he'd trespassed onto private property, Brian took Justine's arm and steered her to a table in the far corner at the front of the café, away from the curious patrons.

Justine immediately lifted a worn plastic menu up to hide her face. "Wow. I guess we should have called ahead and warned them we were coming."

"I think we could have held a parade and gotten the same response. I'm sure everyone in town knows we're here and why."

"Guess they're not happy about it."

Brian looked to the side and the patrons all averted their eyes, except one. He was young, maybe in his twenties, wearing jeans, a red ball cap and a T-shirt with smears of motor oil on it. He stared directly at Brian, as if challenging him to say something. Brian stared right back until the guy looked away. Best to let them know up front that he wouldn't be intimidated.

"This sorta puts a damper on my research," Justine said and sighed.

"You were planning on doing interviews?" It had never occurred to Brian that Justine would talk to the locals.

"I still am, even though it might be hard to get information from them."

"What kind of information do you think they have?"

"Tales mostly. Stories handed down among the generations."

Brian nodded. "I see. You're figuring that the campfire tales and stories used to scare kids might contain an element of truth."

"They usually do."

"That's smart of you and something I never would have thought of."

"Really? I thought cops used rumor and gossip to get leads."

She made an attempt to say it lightly, but Brian caught the underlying animosity and sarcasm in Justine's words. Interesting. Maybe her problem wasn't just with strangers or men, but only with cops. He logged that tidbit for future pondering.

"Yeah, I guess you're right," he said. "It's all hearsay and it's never quite correct, but it's usually enough to send us in the right direction." He was about to ask another question about Justine's research methods, hoping to learn more about his new roommate, when the waitress stepped up to the table.

She was probably in her thirties, but the years of sun and bayou air had weathered her skin, making her look older. Her long, dark hair was piled on top of her head and she looked down at them, brown eyes full of suspicion. "Can I get you something to drink?"

"I'll have sweet tea," Justine said. "My name's Justine and this is Brian."

Justine's introduction clearly surprised the waitress and she bit her bottom lip, the indecision on her face clear as day. "I'm Deedee," she said finally, but Brian could tell she had given the information grudgingly.

"What would you like to drink, sir?" she asked Brian, her eyes fixed on her order pad.

"Sweet tea for me, too."

"Did you want anything to eat?" Deedee asked.

Justine ordered chicken-fried steak and Brian put in an order for a burger and fries. Deedee barely nodded and scurried away from the table, without so much as a glance back. Justine gave Brian a wry smile. "You should really work on your technique. You're scaring all the women away."

Brian saw the cook stop Deedee and ask her a question. Deedee shook her head and started to fill two tall glasses with tea. Her hands shook as she poured the tea from the pitcher into the glasses. Apparently, he wasn't the only one who'd noticed the waitress's discomfort because when she finished pouring, the cook took the glasses and directed Deedee to make more coffee.

Brian sized the man up as he made his way from behind the counter and across the café to their table. He was a big guy, probably in his fifties, and looked as if he could handle most anything life dealt him. He studied them carefully as he walked up to the table, but the fear that Brian saw in the waitress wasn't present in this man.

"Two sweet teas," the cook said and placed the glasses in front of them. "You must be the people that's here to research that house of the damned."

Brian blinked at his rather abrupt, albeit accurate, description. "Yes," he replied and stuck out his hand. "I'm Brian. This is Justine."

"Tom Breaux," the cook said and shook his hand. "I own the café." He pulled a set of keys from his pocket and handed them to Brian. "These are for you. Sammy's house is on the street behind the café, about fifty yards east. Has yellow siding and white trim."

"Thanks," Brian said, and took the keys.

Tom looked at Justine. "What kind of research are you doing?"

"Family stuff mostly," Justine relayed the cover story

she and Olivia had agreed upon, "and furniture cataloging. Antiques are a specialty of mine."

Tom nodded then fixed his gaze back on Brian, narrowing his eyes. "Pardon me if I say so, but you don't look like some brainy researcher." He inclined his head at Justine. "Not that you do either, ma'am."

"I'm not a researcher," Brian said, certain the man had already heard about the sheriff's visit and was fishing for information. It was the setup Brian had been looking for. "I'm more of the freelance security sort."

Tom raised his eyebrows. "Seems a strange place to freelance."

"I'm a friend of Olivia's. She asked me to watch over the repair people she has scheduled, and make sure Justine's work follows an uncomplicated path."

Tom gave a single laugh. "Yeah, well, it's gonna take more than muscle and a keen eye for shooting to best what's going on at that house. You can't shoot or wrestle haunts."

Justine leaned across the table toward Tom. "You really believe the house is haunted?"

"I know it for a fact. Things has gone on out there as long as I lived and a hundred years before. Ain't no human been out there causing trouble for over a hundred years. The place is cursed. I told your friend Olivia the same thing, but she didn't listen. And look what it got her—almost killed by a madman."

"But a *human* madman," Justine pointed out.

Tom shook his head. "The man was cursed. Cursed by the spirits in that house."

"That man was cursed by insanity," Brian said.

"Yeah," Tom agreed, "just like Franklin Borque. I heard all the stories growing up—about why he built that monstrosity in the swamp to hide all the valuables he acquired, some legally, some not—including that wife that he bought and paid for, then stuck out here to die. That attorney may have been cursed with insanity, but it came from that house. Came from the ghost of Franklin Borque."

Brian studied Tom's face, figuring the man was trying to scare them away, but he saw no hint of dishonesty. Clearly Tom Breaux believed everything he'd just said.

"Mr. Breaux," Brian said, "if I didn't know any better, I'd say you were trying to scare us with a ghost story."

Tom shook his head. "And that would be where you're wrong, sir. I'm trying to *warn* you with a ghost story. You should already be scared." He gave them a nod. "Your food will be ready in a couple of minutes."

Brian watched him walk away, then looked over at Justine. "Well, what do you make of that, Madam Researcher?"

Justine watched Tom step behind the counter and say something to Deedee. The woman pulled a cigarette out of her apron and exited the café by the back door, looking completely unnerved. "I think he's lived in these bayous so long, he believes the old stories."

Brian nodded. "That was my read, too, but I'm not willing to cross him off the list. There's a trail behind the caretaker's cottage that leads to a couple of cabins on the bayou that you can only reach by boat. Jake and Olivia saw Tom unloading boxes on the dock."

"Does he live there?"

"According to his driver's license, he's got a house in town, back behind the café, but that doesn't mean he doesn't own a cabin, too."

"Or he's friends or relatives with someone who does," Justine added. "Either way, you're right—he's got access to laMalediction. Is there any way to find out who owns the cabins?"

"John and I didn't have any luck with it. The land's all owned by an estate, and there aren't any leases we could find. But if those cabins have been down there forever, likely no one handling the estate cares. The estate's probably holding the land for mineral rights. A couple of cabins aren't going to hurt anything."

"You didn't tell him you were a cop, either. Still trying to make the sheriff work for his information?"

"Just biding time, really. They can find out easily enough. But I was hoping, if they didn't know right away, I might get some information out of them. Guess that plan failed miserably."

Justine frowned. "That waitress knows something."

"Deedee? That woman is scared of her own shadow. Even if she knew anything, you'd never get it out of her."

"Want to bet? Let me come to breakfast tomorrow morning alone. I'll get something out of her."

Brian's first reaction was to refuse. He didn't like the idea of letting Justine out of yelling range, but the café was a public place, and according to Tom, not far from the rental house. He nodded. "Okay. Tomorrow morning, I'll go shopping for supplies for the rental house and you can take a shot at Deedee."

He felt his neck tingle and knew someone was staring at him. Looking over at the counter, he saw Deedee standing next to the coffeepot and staring in their direction, her expression wary. For a split second, he could have sworn her expression shifted from fearful to cunning, but before he could even blink it was gone. She jerked her head away as soon as he locked eyes with her, but Brian couldn't help but wonder if she'd understood what they were saying.

If so, then Justine needed to be very careful when questioning the waitress, who may not be as helpless as she appeared.

JUSTINE SCANNED THE INSIDE of the rental house with a critical eye. It was small—much smaller than she preferred to share with another person, especially Brian. Standing in the middle of the living room, she could see into every room in the house. Brian, of course, had been tickled with the layout and had immediately set about double-checking locked windows and installing sensors, making the space seem even smaller.

Find a place to work.

If she could get immersed in her work, she'd be able to forget that she was essentially trapped in a condo-size house with a man trained to ferret out people's secrets. There was no desk in either of the tiny bedrooms and no place to fit one, either. The kitchen had a counter with two barstools that would be sufficient for eating but not for spreading out her research. The living room was one big room that contained both living room furniture and a decent-size dining table, so she decided to claim the dining table.

She pulled out the set of journals she brought with her from laMalediction, and her laptop, and got everything arranged on the table so that she could work. Brian had the forethought to purchase a gallon jug of sweet tea from the café, so she poured herself a tall glass and settled into a chair. She'd barely gotten her laptop fired up when Brian came in from his outside security work.

"Not a lot of room in here," he said, looking over at Justine's dining-table setup. "Will you have enough space to work?"

"I think so. We'll be at the house the majority of the day. I'll just bring whatever I'm currently working on here at night. Anything that needs more research will have to wait until the next day."

Brian nodded. "I've got the security system in place.

Let me know when you're taking a break and I'll show you how to work it. I'm going to grab a shower. Ought to be a fast one, as I had to turn on the water heater."

He pulled off his T-shirt as he left the room and Justine couldn't help but notice that the body below the shirt did not fail to impress. As he rounded the corner into the hallway, she got a glimpse of a scar on his lower back, on his side, just above the waistline of his jeans. She'd seen enough hunting accidents to know it was a bullet hole, but Justine didn't think for a minute that Brian had been foolish enough to get shot hunting. Likely, it was either his military service or being a cop that had placed that scar on his back.

She heard the shower fire up in the bathroom and a couple of seconds later, a yowl from Brian, which made her smile. She'd definitely wait a couple of hours for the water heater to do its magic. Her mind flashed momentarily to a vision of Brian, minus the jeans, standing beneath the stream of water, and she forced it to change channels. The very last thing she could afford to do was let her guard down around the one person who had the best opportunity to blow her cover. She'd already lapsed into a level of comfort with him too easily on several occasions.

Picking up the journal on the top of her stack, she focused her attention back on her work. Somewhere in those diaries had to be information on the identity of Marilyn's lover—the man she suspected was her mother's great-great grandfather. All Justine's attempts to locate her mother's family had resulted in dead ends, leaving only this one angle left to investigate. It was the reason she'd jumped at the job when Olivia offered it, and likely her one chance to figure out if the horrible mental illness that consumed her mother was something that had been passed from generation to generation.

Despite Tom Breaux's dire predictions, Justine didn't fear a spirit taking over her body. Her biggest fear was a hereditary mental disorder taking away her sanity. Without knowing if her mother's illness was an isolated case in the family tree, Justine would always live with the fear that under the right circumstances she'd break from reality like her mother did. That fear had kept her isolated, afraid to form close bonds with others. Afraid of the hurt she could inflict on anyone who cared.

She flipped through the pages, looking for an indication of the child and how it came to be, when a passage in Sissy's journal caught her eye.

April 15, 1863
The master returned unexpected last night. He'd been shot in the leg and given a discharge. He limps some, but the leg didn't slow him down any, once he saw what the missus had done. I came to her this morning as I always do. She had already taken all manner of care with her face, but it still didn't hide the master's work.

Justine compared the date with her earlier notes on Marilyn's journals to confirm that both journals referred to Franklin's return from the war. The time lines were the same. Justine knew that Franklin murdered Marilyn only months after his return, so she must have had the child before his return. It was odd though, that Marilyn had never mentioned the child in her own journals.

She scanned a couple more pages in Sissy's journal and her eyes locked on one dated several weeks later.

May 18, 1863
The master told her the child had to go. She tried

to pass him off as a servant's, but the child's green eyes are a perfect match for the mistress and give away her betrayal. The master can't stand the sight of the baby, and truth be, I fear for the child's life. The mistress is beside herself but can't continue to take the beatings. I think she knows he's capable of turning his anger on the child. He was a mean man before, but since his return, he seems to have lapsed further into madness.

I promised the mistress I will send word for my sister in New Orleans to take the child. He has the dark color of the Creoles and the mistress wants him raised among his kind.

I will write my sister tomorrow and hope word reaches her in time.

Justine felt her pulse increase as she read the passage again. Despite her mistress's lack of mention of the child in her own journals, Sissy hadn't seemed to have a problem recording what was going on. At first, Justine had thought Marilyn avoided mentioning the child because she was afraid Franklin would find the journals and discover her secret, but according to Sissy, Franklin had likely known of Marilyn's betrayal from the moment he saw the child.

Maybe it was superstition. That would make sense, given Marilyn's foray into learning voodoo. She might have believed that writing about her son would somehow curse him.

Justine shook her head in frustration. The old ways claimed mystical power, but really seemed to control through fear. Justine's mother was the most fearful person she'd ever known, even in her lucid times. And what about Marilyn's lover? She'd made no mention of him in her journals after the passage that they'd reunited, but if the child was in danger, why not send him to his father?

She reread the passage one last time then made a quick note to pull the next set of Sissy's journals first thing in the morning. It was getting late and she was exhausted. First thing tomorrow morning, she'd pull everything she could about Sissy's sister and Marilyn's lover in order to locate the child...possibly the only link to the rest of her family.

THE INTRUDER WATCHED from the edge of the swamp as the lights in the rental house went off. The attack on the woman apparently hadn't changed their mind about staying. That writer woman had been a big enough nuisance, but he'd thought the crazy attorney had handled that problem for him. Now he had a second woman on his hands, and apparently, one just as stubborn as the first, which was both frustrating and unfortunate.

Frustrating for the intruder because his carefully laid plans were beginning to unravel.

Unfortunate for the woman and the man who wouldn't leave.

Chapter Six

In the middle of the night, the sound of a car alarm sent Brian bolting out of bed for the front door, pistol ready. Justine ran out of her bedroom, right behind him and suitably armed.

"What happened?" she asked.

Brian put his finger to his lips and pointed to the front door. "It's the alarm on my Jeep," he whispered. "Position yourself behind the kitchen counter, and if anyone walks through that door besides me, open fire."

Justine's eyes widened but she nodded and slipped into the kitchen, crouching so that only the top of her head and eyes were visible over the counter. Brian pulled back the curtain covering the window in the front door and peered out into the darkness. He couldn't see anything moving, but that wasn't a surprise in the inky black.

He pulled the dead bolt back and slowly opened the door, pausing for a moment to see if he drew any fire. When none came, he slipped out into the dark and made a dash for Justine's car, parked closest to the door. Peering over the dashboard, he scanned the driveway and street in front of the house. No storm rocked Cypriere tonight, but the clouds covered the moon, eliminating any light source outside the rental home and down the street.

Brian waited several minutes, listening for the sound of

movement, watching for even the slightest variation in the few shadows that he could make out. Finally, he moved from behind Justine's car and around to his Jeep. The night air was still, and the only sounds were the night creatures in the swamp beyond the house. He peered over the hood of his Jeep and realized that the hood seemed to drop off at a slant.

Already knowing what he would find, he rose and walked around the Jeep to study the two flat tires on the driver's side. The perpetrator had probably run as soon as he set off the car alarm. Disgusted, Brian walked back into the house, calling out to Justine as he entered.

"It's Brian. Hold your fire."

A second later the kitchen light came on and Justine stood next to the switch, her pistol still in her hand. It was then that Brian realized she wore only a thin T-shirt and cotton shorts that gave him a long, clear view of her absolutely perfect legs.

"Did you see anything?" she asked.

His thoughts broke off suddenly, which was just as well. The last thing he needed on his mind was Justine's legs, when clearly he had a situation to manage. "Yeah, two flat tires on my Jeep. Apparently, my car alarm interrupted his work."

Justine frowned. "Tire slashing? That seems rather juvenile after the big stunt last night."

Brian nodded. "Yeah. Tonight definitely lacks the planning and finesse the other required. But maybe he's improvising, since last night failed to send us running back to New Orleans."

"Or maybe it's someone else."

"Maybe. But I'm not willing to yell conspiracy just yet."

Justine nodded. "Okay, but I'm keeping the word in

reserve." She looked down at her watch. "Three a.m. Unless you were planning on doing a stakeout the rest of the night, I'm going back to bed." She pressed the safety on her pistol and trudged back to her bedroom.

Brian watched until she closed the door behind her, trying not to think about how her legs looked even better from behind. He went into his own bedroom and shut the door, thinking a second cold shower wasn't really a bad idea.

JUSTINE YAWNED for at least the hundredth time as she walked down Main Street from the rental house to the café. She'd tried to go back to sleep after the alarm incident the night before, but instead, had only ended up tossing and turning the rest of the night, her sleep disturbed by frantic dreams, none of which she could remember that morning.

At least Brian had respected their agreement from the day before and hadn't insisted on accompanying her to the café. Instead, he opted to visit the local mechanic and see if he could help with the tire situation, and then pick up supplies for the rental house at the convenience store in Cypriere. He'd looked a bit surprised at her very minimalistic grocery requirements, but Justine was hardly what one would call domestic. Books had always been far more fascinating than domestic pursuits, and her usual diet consisted of whatever lo-cal microwave dinner was on sale.

The chicken-fried steak from the night before, the lack of sleep and skipping her morning run, were all conspiring to drain her energy levels, but Justine was determined to talk to Deedee, assuming the woman worked that morning.

It was barely 7:00 a.m. when she entered the café, and only a few patrons were inside, which was normal, as most of the townspeople probably made their living in the bayous and would have been at work by daybreak. A couple of old-timers looked curiously at her, but no one froze like they did yesterday.

Deedee barely glanced at Justine as she slid onto a stool at the counter. She watched out of the corner of her eye as the waitress refilled coffee mugs for the regulars. They must have asked about her because Deedee glanced back again, said something brief, then hurried away from their table. Justine couldn't even begin to imagine why her mere presence in Cypriere seemed to have the waitress that much on edge, but she was determined to find out.

Tom Breaux stepped out of the cooler with a slab of bacon and gave her a nod. "Coffee?" he asked.

"That would be great," Justine replied. "And the breakfast special—eggs over easy, please."

Tom passed her the coffee, then cracked a couple of eggs open on the grill and added bread to the toaster. He had that fluid motion when working that told Justine he'd been doing this very thing for a long time. She wondered if he'd spent his entire life in Cypriere, cloaked in superstition and tradition.

"Heard you had some trouble last night," Tom said as he turned from the grill to refill her coffee.

"So soon? Did someone confess over coffee?"

Tom smiled. "It's an hour past daylight. Gossip's been flying here for at least that. No one confessed, but Chris Pauley lives down the street and saw the flat tires on the Jeep when he was on his way here. He owns the mechanic's shop at the end of the street. Figured he'd be seeing your man sometime this morning."

"He's not my man," Justine automatically corrected him. "He's here working, the same as me."

Tom snorted. "Yeah, 'freelancing.' That guy's military or cop or both."

Justine tried to maintain a blank face, hoping to get some information out of the café owner. "Sounds like you're making that observation from experience," she said, neither confirming nor denying Tom's assessment of Brian.

"I did my time in a uniform. No war going on then, at least not on paper, but I saw some action that didn't exactly make it in the history books."

Interesting, and something that elevated Tom from benign café owner to a very real threat. "Let's just say Olivia wanted my stay here to be less adventurous than her own," Justine explained. "Brian's a friend of hers and offered to keep an eye on things while I'm working."

Tom plated her food and slid it in front of her. He glanced to the corner where the old-timers sat, then leaned a bit toward her and lowered his voice. "If she'd really wanted things to be less adventurous, she'd have burned that cursed relic to the ground when she had the opportunity. You watch your back. Ain't no man alive suited to fight what's been awakened at laMalediction."

Tom slipped away from the counter and back into the cooler. Justine stared after him, feeling the hair rise on the back of her neck. What in the world had a hard, tough man like Tom Breaux seen or heard about the house that made him so fearful? And was there a grain of truth in his fear?

She'd tried to dismiss the incident her first night in laMalediction as lack of preparedness on her part for not anticipating an early strike, but all the precautions in the world wouldn't save her from a ghost or a very real stalker. Clearly something was going on in Cypriere—something that someone didn't want discovered.

Justine dug into her breakfast with more fervor than usual and mentally calculated the miles she'd need to run to work off the pile of eggs cooked in bacon grease, but she didn't skip a single bite. She languished over her coffee and kept an eye on Deedee, hoping to catch the waitress slipping out back for a break. Tom refilled her coffee regularly, but remained silent, apparently having said all he needed to say.

Justine was just about to go into coffee overload when Deedee told Tom she was taking her break and headed out the back. Justine waited a minute, then placed some money on the counter and thanked Tom for the breakfast before heading out of the café. She forced herself not to rush as she walked down the sidewalk in front of the plate-glass window of the café, trying to look normal, then slipped around the corner to the alley in the rear.

Deedee sat at a weather-beaten wooden picnic table behind the café, smoking a cigarette. Her head jerked up as Justine stepped on some broken glass, and she stared at Justine with a deer-in-the-headlights look. Justine gave her a wave and casual hello and strolled over to the picnic table, trying to appear nonchalant.

Deedee averted her eyes and placed the cigarette between her lips. Justine noticed her hands shook as she held it in place for a draw. "Deedee, right?" Justine said, trying to sound friendly.

Deedee nodded, but didn't raise her gaze.

Justine stopped in front of the picnic table, deliberately positioning herself in the middle of the walkway between Deedee and the back door of the café. "I'm Justine. We met yesterday."

"I remember," Deedee said, her raspy voice low.

"I'm doing research on the history of the house for the

estate. I wondered if you've lived around here all your life and could tell me some of the local superstitions."

Deedee's eyes widened, and when she looked up, Justine could tell the woman was clearly frightened. "I can't speak of such things," Deedee whispered. She looked nervously up and down the alley, then back at Justine. "Speaking of them gives them power."

"It's just stories and lore, Deedee. Surely you can't believe haunts would come get you if you talk about them?"

Deedee shook her head. "Not me. They'd come for *you*. You're the one they want. I knew it from the first moment I saw you."

Deedee rose from the picnic table and leaned toward Justine. "They got you here, called to you in the night when you were sleeping and got into your mind. They're not going to let you leave until they get what they want."

"Which is what?"

"Renewed energy. You're the one who can sustain them."

Justine stared. "Are you trying to tell me you think the spirits will take my soul to sustain themselves?"

"I don't think—I know. You should get in your car and leave. Forget you ever heard of Cypriere or that cursed house. Put as many miles between you and southern Louisiana as you can manage, and never return as long as you live."

Deedee dropped her cigarette butt on the ground and crushed it out with her foot. She stepped around Justine and hurried back into the café, without so much as a backward glance. Justine stared after her for a minute, then crossed the alley and a vacant lot to the street where the rental house was located.

If Deedee was faking her fear, Justine was impressed.

The waitress had suggested Justine leave immediately and never return. Were her words a threat or a warning? Clearly Deedee was scared of something—the question was whether she was really afraid of spirits and haunts or whether she knew what was going on at laMalediction and was afraid of the person behind it.

Justine blew out a breath of frustration. An hour and a half of digging and she was no closer to a guess on what was at work in Cypriere than she had been before she got here. In fact, if anything, she was more confused. She still had no way to separate imaginary fears from the real ones, nor even a clue as to where to start looking for the very real person who'd slashed Brian's tires and hit her on the head. Spirits didn't slash tires or create the smell of smoke to lure you from a locked room.

Brian pulled into the driveway as she walked up to the rental house, and gave Justine a wave as he climbed out of the Jeep. "You're just in time to help me unload," he said.

Justine pulled a couple of paper bags full of groceries out of the backseat. "I hope you found something healthy. I just ate a month of grease at the café."

"That bad?" Brian asked as he pulled a box of canned goods out of the back of the Jeep.

"No, it was that good. I just can't afford to eat that way every day."

Brian laughed. "I picked up skim milk, granola, wheat bagels and low-fat cream cheese. I was surprised at the selection at the store. They had everything on your list."

"Sounds perfect," she said as they entered the rental house. "So I guess Chris 'The Gossip' Pauley was able to fit you with some tires."

Brian placed the box of groceries on the kitchen counter. "Wow. Word spread that fast?"

"Yep. It's the first thing Tom brought up when I got to the café."

Brian shook his head. "Apparently I underestimated the local news chain."

"Or the boredom level. Probably nothing much out of the ordinary happens here. You and I account for two acts of random violence in as many days."

"True. Chris Pauley was the guy in the café yesterday wearing the ball cap."

"The one with the staring problem?"

"You noticed that, too? Yeah, that's the one."

Justine frowned. "So, did he have anything to say about your tires?"

Brian gave her a wry smile. "Oh, he couldn't stop talking about it. Ran his mouth the entire time he worked."

"And…?"

"We're just bringing more trouble to this town. It had no problems before Olivia came to stay at the devil house, and so on. The gist of it ended with his advice that we leave before we cause doom and gloom to descend on heavenly Cypriere."

Justine nodded. It sounded like the same spiel Deedee had given her but without the spirit- or soul-stealing part. "Speaking of doom and gloom, did you call our friend the sheriff?"

"Oh, yeah. He made an obligatory stop at the mechanic's shop and essentially suggested that if we went back to New Orleans, not only would our problems cease but his would, as well."

Justine sighed. "Seems like a recurring theme." She filled Brian in on her conversations with Tom and Deedee.

"We're not exactly winning any popularity contests here," Brian said. "I expected problems after talking to

John, but I guess I didn't expect this many, this varied, or this soon."

"And the local opposition—were you expecting that?"

"It's pretty much exactly what I expected. We're upsetting the mix. If they believe in the curse nonsense, then they're going to think we're stirring up spirits. If they're involved in something nefarious at laMalediction, we're going to be in their way."

"That's the same conclusion I came to after talking with Tom and Deedee." She stared out the kitchen window for a moment. "I think one or both of them knows something."

"Probably. But whether what they know does us any good or even applies to our situation is a whole other issue. That's the biggest problem with police work. Everyone's hiding something, but so many times it has nothing to do with the crime."

"Everybody has secrets." God knows *she* did.

Brian rubbed his jaw, his expression thoughtful. "Yeah, I suppose you're right. It's just that some people's secrets don't end with murder."

Chapter Seven

Justine put another stack of Sissy's journals on the library table. They'd arrived at laMalediction around noon, given the late start, and Justine had spent another frustrating two hours not finding a single clue about what happened to Marilyn's lover or where Sissy's sister lived or whether Marilyn's child made it safely out of Cypriere.

Despite all the rumor and myth and the obvious local fear of the estate, Justine didn't buy for one minute that an adult male and a child had disappeared into thin air. They went somewhere, but damned if she could find a trace of them so far in the journals.

She opened a bottled water and took a long drink. Her frustration level was growing, and she needed to take a step back and collect herself. It was only her second day on the job, and neither had been a full one. She needed to control her impatience. The answers were in this library, buried on a few pages of the thousands that occupied the shelves. With systematic elimination, she'd eventually find them.

Besides, it wasn't like Olivia had given her a deadline. In fact, Olivia had been quite clear that the job would continue until Justine found the answers the estate attorney required, or she was out of options for further research. A more pressing concern was whether the scare tactics would cease long enough for her to actually do the job.

She reached for another journal and opened it to the first page, but before she could begin reading, the light in the room faded. Dark clouds swirled outside the library window, blocking the sunlight and providing fair warning that a storm was on its way. She barely had a second to wonder if Brian had noticed the storm when he stepped into the library.

"A storm's blowing in," he said. "Came in suddenly off the gulf, but it's not supposed to last. I figured we could wait it out, if that's okay with you."

"That's fine."

"We'll probably lose power," he warned.

"I have about four hours of battery backup on my laptop, and a kerosene lamp, so I'm good for the afternoon anyway."

Brian nodded. "Okay. I'm going to make a quick check of the perimeter of the house. Make sure the alarm is working properly. If it goes off any time in the next ten minutes or so, just ignore it."

"Okay," Justine replied as he hurried off down the hall. She heard the front door open and close, then saw him cross the window in front of the library on his march around the house. She gave the swirling sky one final look, then focused back on the journal in front of her. It was a more recent one, and after the time Justine figured Marilyn had the baby. She hoped Sissy would mention the father.

May 20, 1863

I knew it were wrong, but the mistress couldn't be swayed. We stood there that night in the graveyard, waiting for something that should have

never happened—something that would eventually destroy us all. I took the vow, along with the mistress and the other, and to this day, I have never spoken of that night.

But someone did, and now we'll all pay.

Justine's pulse increased. The graveyard? What the hell were they all doing in the graveyard? She reread the passage to make sure she hadn't misunderstood.

It appeared that Sissy was writing about an event that had happened months or weeks before that was just now coming back to haunt them. But what event had happened in the graveyard? Justine stared out the window, lost in thought. The night Franklin murdered Marilyn, only those two died. She sucked in a breath. Not the child! Was that it? Had Franklin murdered Marilyn's child before Sissy could send him away? Had Marilyn put a curse on Franklin over the grave of her deceased child?

Lightning struck just outside the library window and thunder boomed a split second later, causing her to jump. She felt the room vibrate from the blast and the lights immediately snapped off. She rose from her chair and looked out the library window. The rain blew in sheets across the courtyard, already creating narrow channels in the landscaping bed outside the library. Poor Brian must have gotten caught outside in the downpour.

Movement across the courtyard caught Justine's eye and she squinted into the storm, trying to determine what was out there. Surely Brian hadn't gone across the courtyard to the caretaker's cottage. She watched for a couple of seconds and was just about to decide she'd seen something blowing in the wind, when she saw it again. And this time there was no confusion.

The white-robed figure stood on the far side of the

courtyard behind the fountain. Justine didn't see the glowing red eyes this time, but she couldn't shake the overwhelming feeling that the figure knew she was there and was looking straight at her. She knew the smart thing to do was to back away from the window and pull her gun out of her backpack, but she found herself rooted to that spot, almost as if her shoes were nailed to the floor.

She stared at the figure, praying it didn't come any closer, and at the same time wanting desperately to know what it was and what it wanted. After a couple of seconds, the figure lifted one arm and seemed to point east. Justine looked east, but couldn't make out anything but a wall of cypress trees that covered the swamp. The caretaker's cottage and storage shed were north of the house, not east, and Justine knew of no other outbuilding that the old caretaker had identified as part of the estate.

She looked back to the figure, but it was gone. Pressing her face against the window, she strained to see across the courtyard, to make out where the figure might have gone. She'd only looked away for seconds. How had the figure disappeared completely? Even in the storm, the white robes would glow in the dim light. If the figure was in her line of sight, she would be able to see it.

A burst of lightning lit up the entire courtyard and she quickly scanned every inch of it. There was nothing outside any longer.

Justine backed away from the window and tried to collect her thoughts. Deep in her bones, she felt the figure was trying to tell her something. But what could be out in the swamp?

She glanced down at the table and froze. *The graveyard!*

Because of the remote location of the estate, Franklin Borque would have built a family cemetery somewhere on the property. Even though she had no proof at all, Justine was certain she'd find that cemetery east, in the swamp where the figure had pointed. And the cemetery might contain the information she was looking for. A way to trace her lineage.

Her mind whirled with thoughts. She had to figure out how to get out of laMalediction without setting off an alarm. She wasn't about to tell Brian that the ghostly figure had appeared and pointed her into the swamp. Brian assumed the figure was a person with nefarious intent. He'd insist she was walking into a trap and forbid her to go.

And Justine thought the figure was…what?

She didn't actually know, or she didn't want to admit that for the first time in her life she might actually believe that some things were not of the living.

BRIAN STRUGGLED to pull off his mud-caked boots outside the kitchen entry into laMalediction. The door led straight out of the kitchen and onto the lawn, but contained no awning, so the rain pelted him as he yanked the heavy boots off his feet. By the time he stepped inside the kitchen he was soaking wet.

"You're marring the pristine floor." Justine's voice sounded from the doorway.

"Ha. Yeah, I might create a layer of mud in that dust with all the water I'm shedding."

"Don't move," Justine said. "I'll be right back with some towels."

Brian wiped the water from his forehead and eyes, and a couple of minutes later Justine returned with towels from the upstairs bathroom. "Thanks," he said as he ran the first one across his head to remove the water from his short hair.

"Guess this is one of those times when it pays to have

a military cut," Justine observed. "Was everything okay outside?"

"Everything looked fine. I was hoping I'd beat the storm, but man, it came up fast. John told me the storms seemed to appear at once, but this is still more than I imagined."

Justine nodded. "I think it's because of the swamp. You can't see the skyline much beyond the cleared part of the estate, so the storm's right on top of us before we know it."

"Makes sense." He smiled. "I guess everything has a logical explanation, even the things that happen here."

Justine didn't answer immediately. "We can only hope."

"Don't tell me this place is getting to you already?"

"No. Not the place, but a combination of Olivia's dreams, the stories in the journals and something floating outside in a downpour in the middle of the night is enough to make you wonder. I mean, I've never come out and said that certain things don't exist, but I've never seen proof of them, either."

Brian considered her words. "I see what you mean. I'm certain Olivia's telling the truth about her dreams, but I can't think of another explanation for them than that she's somehow dreaming the past."

Justine nodded. "Especially when you consider that she's been having those dreams her entire life, but didn't find out the story of laMalediction and Marilyn Borque until recently. It makes even a skeptic wonder, more so when you have as credible a person as Olivia."

"Yeah, but a bad dream didn't crack you on the back of the head or slash my tires. Which reminds me..." He turned and punched in a code on the alarm pad next to the kitchen door. "If an exterior door opens, a window is lifted anywhere on the first level of the house or someone opens the basement door, this alarm will sound off, and I mean loud."

He reached for a black object on the kitchen counter that looked like a remote. "This has every alarm point noted on it," he said, pointing to a row of labels next to a green light. "As long as that location is secure, the light is green. If the location is breached, the light turns red."

"What about the contractors who are scheduled to come?"

"John wants me to personally escort every contractor during their tour of the house, so I'll be able to control the alarm. Once Olivia gets all the bids, John will run extensive background checks on anyone they want to hire. We'll deal with the actual work issues when the time comes, but that will probably take a couple of months. With any luck, you'll find the emeralds and be back home by then."

"With any luck," Justine agreed.

He handed the security sensor to Justine. "Keep this with you at all times. The alarm will let you know immediately if security is breached, but this will tell you where. Get as far away from the breached location as possible without leaving the house, and I will find you. Do not attempt to investigate. That's my job."

"Sure," Justine said. "I'm going to get some more work done before my battery's dead."

Brian nodded. "I'm going to change shirts and start working on furniture inventory upstairs. Don't be alarmed if you hear me banging around up there."

"No problem," Justine said, and left the kitchen.

Brian watched her walk down the hallway and into the library and wondered again what the quiet beauty was thinking. In conversation she seemed so direct, but Brian always sensed that she was holding something back...that her mind was whirling in a million directions that she wasn't about to share with someone else.

The question was, did it have anything to do with laMalediction?

JUSTINE STARED DOWN at the sensor, feeling the walls of the house close in around her. This was far more than she had expected in security. This was state-of-the-art and not anything a layman could get around without some work. She stared across the estate grounds to the swamp east of the house. So close, but yet technologically, out of her grasp. Damn it. She had to find some way around Brian's high-tech security.

He hadn't said anything at all about seeing the figure across the courtyard, so either he'd been in a different area of the estate or he hadn't noticed it in the storm. *Or it wasn't really there.* She shook her head, warding off that thought. It wasn't productive. Brian saw the white-robed figure on their first night in Cypriere. The figure was real. Whether it was a real person or not was the question.

Sighing, she flopped into her chair and pulled a journal off the stack. There was no use dwelling on it now. She'd figure out something tonight and come back tomorrow with a plan. In the meantime, she needed to make some notes on her research before her battery ran out. She flipped through the pages of the journal, scanning the entries. This journal was much earlier than the others, and she tried to place the date in her time line of events. It was after Franklin left for war and before he returned, but Justine was trying to determine where it fit in the time line of Marilyn's pregnancy.

So far, neither journal had made mention of her pregnancy, and Justine found that odd, especially as the journals were written by the pregnant woman and her personal servant, another woman. A pregnancy was just the sort of thing a woman would usually journal about, and the absence of comments put her senses on high alert that something wasn't quite right.

She scanned the entries that Sissy wrote about gardening and her worries about the weather in the coming winter in such an isolated location. She wrote of long days of polishing silver with her mistress, or sewing in front of the firelight at night.

Justine stopped and reread a passage again. Not just sewing. Sissy specifically made mention that she was "letting out" the mistress's dresses. Granted, everyone could gain weight, but Justine couldn't help but think this might be the start of Marilyn's pregnancy. The question was, how far along was she? Given the tight-fitting dresses of that era, she may have only been a month or two along; but if she starved herself or carried the baby low, she could have been several months along before showing.

She scanned the entries afterward, but no other mention of dresses or Marilyn's size was mentioned. She flipped the last page of the journal over and stared. Something didn't look right. Running her finger down the center of the journal, she could feel the tiny remnants of torn paper. Someone had removed pages from the journal. Certainly not Olivia, and the old caretaker had gladly turned his ancestor's journals over for their research. So who? Were the pages torn recently or had they been missing for decades?

A thud from upstairs reminded her that Brian was working above her and an idea for circumventing the security system flashed through her mind. Several windows on the second floor had tiny balconies. All she needed was a sturdy rope and a small window of opportunity to get out of laMalediction. Tonight, she'd direct dinner conversation around Brian's plans for tomorrow—find out where he would be working in the house. Then she'd make her exit on the other side.

She had to find the graveyard. If the child was buried there, her personal quest at laMalediction was over, even if her job for Olivia wasn't.

BRIAN POSITIONED HIMSELF on the side of a giant bookcase to slide it from its resting spot in the center of the inside wall. When he and John had scoured the rooms weeks before, looking to close off any secret access to the house, he didn't remember the bookcase being in that location but that didn't mean it hadn't been there. The old house had a ton of rooms full of old, dusty furniture and there was no way Brian could remember them all. At least this bookcase was empty, which made the entire moving process a bit less cumbersome.

He placed furniture sliders under each corner of the bookcase and pressed his shoulder into the massive wood structure, pleasantly surprised when it slid easily across the hardwood flooring. When he'd completely revealed the section of wall behind the bookcase, he stopped for inspection.

Running his hands across the wall, he checked every square inch of the old wallpaper for a gap or tear—any sign that a portion of the wall moved. The surface appeared to be solid, but that wasn't necessarily conclusive. Whoever had designed the panels had been a master craftsman. Brian had never seen such seamless work, even though he'd spent a couple of summers working for a cabinetmaker.

Time for another tactic.

He pulled out his tape measure and measured the distance from a window on the back wall of the room to the interior wall in question. Six inches. Then he went into the room next door and measured the distance from that window to the other side of the interior wall. Six inches. He lifted the window and leaned outside, extending his tape measure to the edge of the window in the other room.

Give or take an inch, the windows were two feet apart. That left one foot of space or less between the two rooms. Hardly enough for a passageway, unless one was very slight. He walked back into the other room and retrieved his notebook from the dresser. The room appeared secure, but something about it still bothered him. He flipped to the back of the notebook and opened a pouch taped to the inside of the back cover.

John had taken pictures of each of the rooms to help with the inventory. Maybe something in a photo could help him pin down the inconsistency he felt was there. He flipped through the photos until he found one with the same empty bookcase. He held the photo up next to the bookcase to ensure it was the same piece of furniture. It matched exactly.

When he stepped back to look at the wall and bookcase, he realized that, in the photo, the bookcase was in almost the exact location as it was now, but that wasn't right. He'd moved the bookcase at least three feet down the wall to expose the area behind it. No one had authorized access to the house but him, John, Olivia and now Justine. He'd be willing to bet that none of them had moved the bookcase.

But someone had.

The question was why?

Chapter Eight

Justine polished off her plate of spaghetti and leaned back in her stool at the rental-house kitchen counter with a satisfied sigh. "That was fabulous. But oh, my God, I am going to have to run tomorrow. Since I've been here, I've eaten nothing but yummy, fattening things." She didn't add that the fact that the delicious meal had been prepared by a man who looked more suited to camouflage than a cooking apron invoked feelings deep within her that she didn't want to address.

Brian studied her for a moment, and Justine got the impression he was searching for something.

"What's wrong?" she asked, uncomfortable with his scrutiny.

He broke eye contact and shook his head. "Sorry. I didn't mean to stare, but for a moment, something about you seemed familiar. I guess I zoned out."

Justine felt her heart pound in her chest. She knew exactly what had set him off. The one and only time she'd seen Brian Marcentel before Cypriere, she'd eaten spaghetti with his family. She hastily grabbed for a piece of the pie he'd cut earlier and tried to maintain her cool. "I get that sometimes," she said, happy that her voice wasn't shaking. "I guess I have one of those faces."

"Guess so," Brian agreed and took a huge bite of his pie.

Justine relaxed a bit when it seemed that he'd dismissed the entire incident. "I can't believe you bought pie," she said. "Like the rest of the food wasn't enough."

Brian polished off another bite of pie and nodded. "I know. I'm overdue for some exercise, too. If you don't mind, I'd like to jog at laMalediction—at least around the perimeter of the estate. I want to see if I can locate other trails that might lead to the house."

"Sounds like a plan," Justine said, struggling to contain her elation. Brian was giving her exactly what she wanted—access to the outside of laMalediction. With any luck, she'd be able to spot a good entry place into the swamp on the east side of the estate. At the very least, she'd get to inspect the grounds on the north side of the estate for footprints, just in case her visitor yesterday wasn't really the ethereal type.

"How's the inventory going?" she asked, fishing for more information.

"Fine."

Justine studied his face for a second, curious about his tone. It was short and dismissive, as if there was something he didn't want to talk about. "You find any more secret passageways?" she asked, pressing for more information.

"No," he said, somewhat hesitantly.

"You don't sound entirely certain."

"Maybe I'm not. I found a bookcase that had been moved from its original location, but there's not enough space behind it for a passageway."

"So someone else moved the bookcase before we got here, apparently looking for something. But there's no passageway there, and you and John sealed the existing ones, right?"

"I guess. But the first night we were in the house, everything was locked tight. I know the alarm wasn't up, but I checked the windows and doors. They were all locked from the inside before we went to bed. Your attacker got in the house somehow."

"Unless he was already there," Justine suggested.

"Perhaps. But then, how did he get out and lock the doors behind him?"

"What if he didn't? I mean, what if the basement contains tunnels and rooms that you and John didn't discover? Someone could hide out there for an indefinite amount of time."

"Yeah," Brian said and sighed, his frustration evident.

Justine suddenly realized that his dismissive answer earlier had been Brian's way of protecting her…of preventing her from worrying. "Hey," she said, "please don't feel like you have to keep things from me. I prefer to face things head-on. Besides, knowing everything I'm up against keeps me more alert."

Brian frowned and stared at the wall behind her for a couple of seconds. Finally, he looked back at her and nodded. "You're right. I was only keeping things from you because I don't want anything to interfere with your work. I didn't mean anything personal against you."

"I know. But it's important that we work together on this."

Brian raised his eyebrows. "Really? I got the impression that you liked to work alone and pretty much be left alone."

"That's true, and no, I don't want you standing guard in the library or sitting in a corner of my bedroom watching me sleep. But with both of us keeping an eye out, we have a better chance of catching this guy."

"All right, then. First thing tomorrow, we jog the perimeter of the estate and look for secondary access points."

"What do we do if we find one? I mean, if we find a trail, do we go down it like Olivia and John did on the trail to the cabins?"

"Yeah. If it looks passable and it's not pouring rain, then we should check out anything available." He looked her straight in the eye. "I know I don't have to say this, but make sure you keep your weapon handy at all times."

Justine nodded and rose from her chair. "I'm stuffed and dead tired. If you don't mind, I'm going to put away these dirty dishes, catch a shower and then hit the sack."

"I'm right behind you," Brian said.

Justine made quick work of the dirty dishes, but lingered just a bit in the shower. She would have stayed even longer, but worried that the hot water might run out if she stayed in for too long. She slid on her yoga pants and T-shirt and wrapped a towel around her wet hair before exiting the bathroom.

"It's all yours," she called to Brian, who was watching the news on the television in the living room. He gave her a wave before she stepped into her bedroom and closed the door behind her.

She towel-dried her hair in front of the mirror over the dresser and ran a comb through her long locks. Then she applied lotion to her face and hands, the usual extent of her beauty regimen, and pulled her d[illegible] hair back in a ponytail. As she reached to turn off the lamp on the end of the dresser, she noticed something in the reflection of the mirror. Something on her bedroom window.

She whirled around to look at the window and placed a

hand over her mouth to stifle a scream. Rubbed in the dirt and grime of the window glass were the words *I know.*

Justine rushed to the window and pulled the heavy curtain across it. The words hadn't been there when she'd opened the curtains that morning, she was certain. Pulling back the curtain a tiny bit, she peeked out into the darkness, wondering if someone was out there, waiting for her to see the words. Waiting for her reaction.

She let the curtain slide back into place and crawled into bed, leaving the lamp on, then checked the clip on her pistol and positioned the gun on the nightstand for easy access. Maybe her stalker would see the lamp remain on all night and know he'd unnerved her. Maybe he'd think she would reconsider working at laMalediction.

Maybe he'd picked the wrong woman to mess with.

JUSTINE STRUGGLED to contain her excitement as she and Brian stretched in the courtyard of laMalediction, preparing for their morning run. She'd managed to leave the rental house that morning while Brian was showering, under the guise of retrieving something from her car, but she'd actually spent the minutes removing the message from her bedroom window before Brian discovered it.

Now her mind raced with the possibilities that could come with discovering the family graveyard. Probably she shouldn't look so happy to exercise. That might appear suspicious, given that most people didn't smile when they were about to jog through a marsh at 7:00 a.m.

"Ready?" Br[illegible] asked.

Justine nodd[illegible]

"I'll set my p[illegible]ack [illegible]it. Let me[illegible] if it's too fast or too slow for y[illegible]."

Justine fell in beside him as he set a moderate pace that wasn't going to burn off last night's dinner, but allowed her ample opportunity to scan the grounds for footprints and the edge of the swamp for paths. Brian kept his focus on the ground as well, and Justine relaxed a bit, figuring with both of them on the lookout, if there was anything to find, they'd see it.

They jogged toward the north end of the estate first and Brian pointed to the trail behind the caretaker's cottage—the one that Olivia and John had discovered during their time at laMalediction that led to cabins on the bayou. They continued their sweep of the grounds west, and Justine tried to hold in her frustration that the direction she wanted to look most would be the last ground they covered. Even though the estate hadn't been kept up to livable standards for years, the old caretaker had still managed to keep quite a bit of acreage around the estate clear. It was a good ten minutes before they jogged toward the stretch of swamp that Justine had been waiting to see.

The markings of the trail were immediately visible. With brush so dense, the narrow channel was obvious. Brian drew up short just as Justine spotted the trail and pointed. He pulled the brush back and checked the ground for footprints, but the dirt displayed only jagged lines.

"He wiped his footprints away with brush," Brian said.

Justine nodded. "Not something an innocent person takes the time to do."

"No. Looks like we may have found our entry point."

Justine scanned the distance from the north side of the courtyard to where they stood. "Then [illegible] did he get from here [illegible] back of the courtyard [illegible] night without us seeing [illegible] ing tracks? Not to men[illegible] [illegible]cled the east side of the courtyard. [illegible] would have seen him if he'd tried to cross the estate, even in the storm."

Brian glanced at the courtyard, then looked back at the trail. "Yeah, that white robe seemed to glow, but what if he took off the robe and shoved it in a black bag? He could have slipped by me in the storm if he was wearing dark colors."

"And not left footprints?"

"Yeah, that's the big catch. The footprints could have easily been washed away overnight, but I should have found some behind the fountain."

"Maybe it was some sort of illusion."

He frowned. "You're not buying into the ghost thing now, are you?"

"No, I mean like an optical illusion, where it looked like he was standing behind the fountain but he was really further back."

"I checked for prints on all the ground between the fountain and the swamp, and around the edge of the swamp."

"Then I don't know, unless we have David Copperfield running loose in the Louisiana swamps."

"Well, let's check this trail first, and if we don't find anything, I'll call David's people when we get back to the house."

Justine laughed. "Sounds like a plan."

His expression grew serious and he pulled out his pistol. "Just in case."

She pulled her pistol from her ankle holster and stepped into the swamp behind him. *Just in case.*

Justine estimated they'd been following the almost indiscernible path about one hundred yards into the swamp when they stepped into a small clearing, about ten feet square. Brian pointed to the right.

"You check that side," he said, "I'll check the other."

She followed the clearing around to the right, scanning into the brush and inspecting the ground, looking for another path. About midway down the side, she saw leaves on a bush that were dying. Granted, it was winter and everything was beginning to die, but these leaves were slightly more curled than the brush around it. As if they'd been pulled out of the ground and placed there to hide something. *A path!*

Justine peered into the swamp beyond the dying brush, trying to see signs of a graveyard, but the swamp was too dense to see beyond twenty feet or so. Still, she thought she caught a glimpse of something large and gray, but with all the winter colors in the swamp, she couldn't be certain.

"Anything?"

Brian's voice sounded behind her and caused her to start. "No," she said, and moved past the spot with the dead brush. If Brian found out that she was looking for the graveyard, he'd insist on going with her. She couldn't afford to have him looking over her shoulder as she tried to unravel her family tree. Couldn't afford for him to find out that her main reason for thinking the graveyard was in this area of the swamp was because she'd seen a ghost.

If Brian started wondering about her mental health, he might remember why she looked familiar to him. That was a risk she couldn't afford to take. She finished covering her area of the clearing and met Brian back in the middle.

"I didn't see anything," Brian said, the disappointment in his voice clear. "This clearing doesn't look natural, so why is it here?"

Justine studied the dirt beneath her feet. "There really should be ground cover like everywhere else," she agreed. "Maybe someone had a tent back here that killed the ground cover. Maybe Wheeler was hiding here in a tent, not a fixed structure."

"Then how did Wheeler get back and forth from New Orleans to this site without someone seeing him? He could hardly park in the courtyard of laMalediction and walk around. And if Wheeler used a tent, where is it now? Should we assume he removed it right before he was killed? Dying wasn't part of his plan, so I don't know that he'd have hidden all traces of his hiding place beforehand."

"I don't have an answer. Nothing seems to add up."

Brian looked back down the trail to the estate grounds. "The only thing I can figure is he came in on the other trail from the boat dock. At night, he could have skirted the estate grounds until he made it here. But why go out of his way to hide here when he could have stayed off the other trail?"

"Maybe the other people who own those cabins creep around the woods and he was afraid he'd get caught. For that matter, wouldn't one of them have reported Wheeler using the docks after he was killed?"

"Unless someone was in on it with him."

"You think Tom Breaux could be?"

Brian stared into the swamp for several seconds and finally blew out a breath. "It would certainly make things easier to understand if that were the case—logistically anyway. But it makes no sense from the other perspective."

"What do you mean?"

"Tom Breaux warned Olivia away from the house, just like he warned us away. Wheeler trapped Olivia here so she couldn't leave. If Tom was working with Wheeler, why would he encourage Olivia to go?"

Justine shook her head. "I have no idea." Brian was right. The entire situation didn't add up.

"Is this what your job is always like?" she asked. "A bunch of things that look like clues, a bunch of things that don't and none of them seem to be part of the same picture?"

"Fortunately, no. Most criminals are not very smart, and their motives are easy to identify. It's the long-term criminals that are more difficult to ferret out. There are so many layers, and sometimes multiple objectives."

"Long-term criminals with multiple objectives—that certainly sounds like what's going on here."

Brian gave her a rueful smile. "Guess Olivia and John aren't getting the answers they want anytime soon." He glanced once more around the clearing then looked back at her. "Well, there's nothing else to do here, and I'm sure you need to get to work. We should head back to the house."

Justine stepped behind Brian and followed him down the trail to the estate grounds. She'd worked hard to contain her excitement during their conversation, but now all she could think about was getting back into the swamp to investigate that opening in the brush. It had to be the graveyard. Maybe Wheeler had a temporary camp here because he thought the emeralds were in the graveyard and he came when he could to search.

Justine always carried emergency supplies in her car and had stashed a long length of rope in her backpack that morning. Maybe some of the answers she was looking for were hidden in that swamp.

Chapter Nine

Brian and Justine grabbed a quick breakfast after their jog, before preparing to start their respective duties. Brian was disappointed that their jog hadn't yielded more information, but reminded himself that he'd only been at it for a couple of days. Unfortunately, the rest of his day would center around furniture inventory and not investigating. He picked up the sensor from the library table and pressed in the code to arm the alarm system.

"I'll be working upstairs on the west side of the house, if you need me," he said. "Are you breaking for lunch?"

Justine glanced at her watch and shook her head. "I'll probably just grab a sandwich and work through. I keep feeling like I should be further along than I am."

"Sounds good. There's a storm moving in late this evening, so I figure we should head out of here by six at the latest, but I'll keep my radio on and listen for changes."

"That's fine."

Brian gave the library one final glance, making sure everything looked in place. "Then I'll get out of your hair."

He left the library and continued upstairs, but a nagging feeling that he'd missed something persisted. Had he missed something on their jog? A trail perhaps? But as he recounted the jog in his mind, he couldn't think of a single place where he might have faltered in his review of the terrain.

Which meant the only other thing that could come under question was Justine. Something about her wasn't quite right in his mind, but he couldn't place what. Certainly she was guarded, but that wasn't the issue. He understood guarded and often practiced it himself, both professionally and personally. And he was certain she was who she claimed to be. He'd seen her published articles and contributions to books, along with the photos to match, and so far, she'd given no indication that she was doing anything but the job she was hired for, except for when she was helping him.

So what was the problem?

That was the sixty-four-thousand-dollar question, and one for which he had no answer. He grabbed a bottled water from the refrigerator in the kitchen, and his notebook, and headed upstairs to continue with the furniture inventory. Right now, he needed to focus on making a list of everything for the appraiser to review. The appraiser was scheduled to visit laMalediction the following week, and he needed to have the list ready as a starting point for the appraiser's work.

That shifted bookcase still bothered him. There was no way a passage could be located in such a narrow space, so why shift the furniture? The only thing he could think of was that someone else had been in the house, looking for passageways, like him. But who? Obviously, not someone who was already in the know; and why would anyone take a chance at entering the house now, when it was under so much scrutiny after Olivia's ordeal?

Nothing made sense. Nothing at all.

Brian was beginning to regret coming to Cypriere. Not only did he feel as if he wasn't making progress on locating the passageways, he was doing a poor job of protecting Justine and their belongings. Not even three full days in Cypriere, and he'd had his tires slashed, and the person he was supposed to be protecting was lured into a trap and knocked unconscious. When all this was over, he might need a vacation from his vacation. Maybe he was losing his edge—getting too personally involved, when he needed to take a professional approach to the situation.

He flipped the notebook open and entered the bedroom at the end of the hall. Standing around wasn't going to sort out his personal issue or get the work done. He gave the room a cursory scan to get a feel for it, then checked the list of items John had recorded for that room—two bookcases, one four-poster bed, two nightstands, one decorative table with a pink vase. Everything seemed in order. He pulled the photos of the room from the envelope in the back of the notebook and checked the photos against the furniture.

It was off.

He faced the wall with the bed and tried to match the placement of the bed and nightstands with the striped wallpaper behind it. The bed was a foot over from where John had photographed it. But why? The bed stood against an exterior wall. There was no way a passageway could be contained behind it.

He stared at the bed for a moment, then a thought hit him. The bed couldn't be hiding a passageway, but something may be contained in a hiding place in the floor beneath the bed. He'd left the furniture sliders in the last room he'd worked in, so he headed down the hall to the east wing of the house to retrieve them to move the bed. He removed the sliders from underneath the bookcase and turned to leave the room, when something moving outside the bedroom window caught his eye.

He rushed to the window and peered outside just in

time to see Justine slip into the swamp on the east side of the estate where they'd searched the trail this morning. His pulse began to race as his emotions shifted from fear to anger. How had she circumvented his security system? And more importantly, why? He tossed the sliders on the bookcase and rushed down the stairs. It took only a couple of seconds to disarm the alarm, and then he bolted out the front door for the swamp.

He glanced back at the house as he jogged across the estate and pulled up short to get a better look at something. A door to the tiny balcony off a second-floor bedroom was open and a rope dangled from the balcony railing. He felt the blood rush up his face as he hurried to the trail. Justine better have a damned good explanation for her actions.

Not that he could think of a single one.

He located the trail they'd investigated before, and stepped into the swamp. Justine was nowhere in sight, but the trees and brush were thick, and she had a jump on him. Why go down this trail again, when they'd already searched it? Unless she'd found something and hid it from him, but why would she do that? Justine was here to do a job, and he was here to protect her. Why would she hide anything from him?

Unless she wasn't who she claimed to be. Unless her reason for being at laMalediction was for some other purpose than Olivia hiring her.

He stopped in the clearing they'd discovered earlier, and slowly walked around the side Justine had inspected. Nothing stood out on his first pass, but when he made a second pass, he saw a broken branch on a bush a couple of feet beyond the clearing. He stepped toward the broken branch and realized the brush beneath his feet was loose and had been cleverly placed to hide a barely visible trail that led deep into the swamp.

He pulled his pistol from the waistband of his jeans and pushed through the dense undergrowth that almost covered the trail. Whatever had possessed Justine to venture out here without him, he hoped it hadn't been a trap.

JUSTINE CREPT DOWN the hidden trail, careful to listen as she progressed. So far, there had been no sign that anyone else occupied this area of the swamp with her, but she wasn't foolish enough to let her guard down. Every time leaves rustled or a bird chirped, she paused, waiting to see if the sound of a human pursuer followed.

She'd continued on the trail about fifty yards deeper into the swamp when she came to a dead end. A thick hedge of brambles rose in front of her and stretched out a good ten feet in each direction. Dismayed, she reached for a stick and tried to push some of the thick brush aside. If this trail turned out to be nothing more than a deer poacher's secret pathway, she was going to be very disappointed.

She peeked through a hole in the brambles and caught a flash of something gray and solid. Her pulse quickened. It looked like a stone structure. A wealthy Louisiana family would definitely have a mausoleum. After a cursory inspection of her options, she pushed through the brush to her left and followed the hedge of brambles to the end, and could hardly contain her excitement as she peered around the end of the hedge.

She'd found the graveyard.

A wrought-iron fence circled the graveyard, leaning in some places but still standing. Several crypts rose out of the bayou earth and littered the tiny graveyard. The largest and fanciest in the center of the graveyard must belong to the Borque family. The smaller ones were probably for generations of valued servants.

She wrestled some with the rusty latch on the gate and

pushed it open. It screeched in protest, and she froze as the sound echoed through the otherwise silent swamp. When she was satisfied that only the bayou creatures had heard the creaking gate, she slipped inside the graveyard and eased it closed behind her.

She scanned the lettering on the front of the smaller mausoleums, and recognized one as Sissy's family surname. The rest weren't known to her, but she hadn't yet compiled a list of all the servants. Likely, she'd find the names somewhere on that list, once it was compiled. She could feel her breath catch in her throat as she approached the big mausoleum in the center of the graveyard. It was probably twenty feet square and eight feet tall at the highest pitch of the sloped roof. The entire structure was carved granite, fashioned to appear as inset columns with an ornate arch.

Even though age and weather had taken its toll on the structure, Justine could see some of the detailed work in the arch that hadn't been eroded by the torrential rainstorms. In tucked away areas the granite shined, and Justine knew at one time the entire structure had been polished to a high sheen that would have felt like glass.

In scrolled lettering across the base of the arched section was the family name Borque. Justine reached up and ran her hand across the grooved lettering, then drew it quickly back, surprised that the stone had been cold to the touch despite the warmth and humidity of the bayou. Even though winter was approaching, it was still a tepid eighty-five degrees.

She placed her hand on one of the columns and drew it back again. Still cold. Despite the bayou heat, she felt a chill run through her and crossed her arms in front of her chest. Immediately, she chided herself for her lapse. *It's just stone. It can't harm you.*

But what is contained inside might.

The thought ripped through her consciousness, but rather than hearing her own voice, it was the voice of her mother that whispered the words in her mind. Justine knew her mother would tell her to leave this place…that evil called this place home, and if disturbed, would attach to her.

But the answer you seek may lie inside these walls.

This time her voice spoke. The voice of reason. The voice of discovery.

Justine took a deep breath and blew it out slowly to steady her body and focus her mind. Even though the structure appeared completely solid, the crypt must have an opening. Somewhere on the outside surface was a lever that would open it. She took one final breath and reached up with one hand and felt the grooved carving at the top of the arch. She pressed each indentation and protrusion with her fingers, looking for the spot that wasn't solid. As she reached the rim of the etching, she realized that the ornate scrolling contained an image within it. She pushed up on her toes, trying to determine what the image represented.

The lion.

Excitement coursed through her body. Inset in the carvings was a cleverly hidden etching of a lion. An etching that matched the description of the lion statue with emerald eyes that Franklin Borque had brought to laMalediction. A quick inspection of the other side of the arch revealed no lion in the scrolling. That had to be it. The lever must be contained within the lion.

She ran her fingers across the surface of the lion. The entire etching was no bigger than two inches square, but as she pressed each spot on the lion, she grew more frustrated when nothing happened. Finally, she dropped her hands and took a step back. She was missing something. Something simple.

She looked across the front of the crypt, up and down each column, and her gaze came to rest at the bottom of an interior column. There appeared to be a hairline crack at the bottom of the column. She reached down and pulled at the edge of the column with her fingers and was surprised when a solid piece of perfectly square granite detached from the column and fell off in her hand.

The granite was so perfectly square, there was no doubt it had been cut in that fashion, and suddenly she knew exactly why. Reaching up, she pressed the granite square flat against the etched lion and immediately, a square piece of the marble shifted back and a panel of granite at the front of the crypt slid open.

She'd had the forethought to bring her flashlight as well as her pistol, so she pulled the flashlight from the back pocket of her jeans and shined the light inside the crypt. It was divided into two sides by a walkway that started at the opening and ended at the back wall. Each side of the crypt contained vaults with the names of those contained inside.

Shining her light on the first row of vaults, she stepped inside the crypt to read the names. The set closest to the opening were the more recent inhabitants of laMalediction and not of interest at the moment, so she moved down to the next section of vaults. She'd just bent over to read a name on a lower vault when she heard footsteps outside the crypt.

She bolted for the opening but was too late. The granite door slid silently into place, leaving her with only her tiny flashlight against the pitch-black tomb. She pushed against the solid granite door, but it wouldn't budge even a hair. Stepping back from the door, she took a deep breath and tried not to panic. There had to be a switch on the inside, right? Surely Franklin wouldn't have built a mausoleum with no backup plan, in case someone was locked inside.

But even if she figured a way out, the person who'd closed her inside was still out there.

She blew out a breath and tried to stop the barrage of information flying through her mind. *Focus on one thing at a time. You have your pistol. Find the way out of here first, and then be prepared to shoot whoever is waiting for you.*

Unless they left you here to die.

She shook her head, trying to block that thought from her mind. There was another way out. She wouldn't even consider an alternative. She guided the light from her flashlight around the perimeter of the opening, hoping to find a lion etching that would indicate the presence of a lever. But the inside contained no etching at all.

Her stomach felt like solid lead had been pumped into it as she slumped against the unmoving door and slid to the ground. She'd made a horrible mistake in not telling Brian her suspicions about the graveyard. The risk of exposing herself was far less than the situation she was now in, and in her frenzy for answers, she'd forgotten to think logically. What a fool she'd been.

Get a grip!

There had to be a way out. She didn't know exactly why, but somewhere within her was a certainty that her life was not supposed to end this way. If she couldn't find a lever, she'd try breaking through the ceiling with the front off of a vault. The ceiling wouldn't be as thick as the sides, and with any luck, may be worn some by weather. Of course, that was assuming she could pry the front off a vault and that she could actually lift it over her head, but she wasn't going to think about that now.

She rose from the ground and pointed her flashlight at the top of the opening, studying every nick and mark on the granite for a sign of the elusive lever. Running her fingers lightly across the surface, she tried to detect any variation that might indicate a break in the seemingly solid slab. As she covered the door inch by inch, worry crept back in, strengthening with every unsuccessful minute.

When she'd finished searching the entire wall, she leaned back against it, took a deep breath and blew it out slowly, trying to maintain some level of calm. It wasn't working. She was going to have to try to break her way out of the crypt, and could only hope and pray that she had the strength and the time to do so. If the crypt was airtight, she had a limited amount of air available. Leaning forward, she inspected the granite marker on the front of the vault. If she could open one and pry the front off, she could use it to break through the roof.

She wasn't going to think about what she might find inside the vault when she opened it.

Positioning her fingers around the edges of the vault facing, she prepared to pull, but as her fingers tightened around the edges, she heard a noise outside. Frozen in place, she strained to make out the sound. It sounded like footsteps on the dying brush that covered the graveyard. She felt her blood run cold, and wondered who stood on the other side of the door, waiting for the right time to kill her.

Chapter Ten

Brian stared in amazement at the graveyard. Logically, he should have known the estate would contain a family cemetery, but his mind still hadn't processed all the historical implications of the house and its history. This must be what Justine had been looking for when she'd snuck out. But why all the secrecy? Given her task at laMalediction, it made perfectly good sense that Justine would want to explore the family graveyard, and he would have gladly accompanied her here.

He studied the ground at the gate opening and found a print that was probably made by Justine's tennis shoes. Stepping through the gate, he glanced around the graveyard but didn't see her anywhere. He looked at the ground again, but the muddy area at the gate was quickly replaced by brush and the footprints disappeared.

"Justine?" he called out. Surely, she would answer, now that he'd caught her.

But not even a breath of air answered his call.

He frowned and scanned the perimeter of the graveyard. It didn't appear to be very large, maybe half an acre. Even if she was behind one of the mausoleums where he couldn't see her, she should have heard him call.

Unless she's unconscious.

His mind flashed back to the first night at laMalediction

that had ended with Justine knocked out by the intruder. Had she been tricked into coming to the graveyard? Was she here but unable to hear him or answer? A small wave of fear passed over him and he worked to squelch it. Now was not the time to think about what could happen. It was time for action.

If he were Justine, what would he have focused on in the graveyard? The most likely answer was the Borque family. He scanned the graveyard again and settled on the largest crypt in the yard. That had to be it.

He crossed the graveyard to the crypt and stood in front of the columned front. The earth in front of it was bare in spots, and he could make out the same tennis-shoe prints he'd found at the gate.

And one other.

His eyes widened and he squatted down to make sure he wasn't wrong in his assessment, but up close, he was even more certain than before. A single, clear bootprint was pressed into the soft earth next to the multiple tennis-shoe prints. By the condition of the prints and the surrounding earth, he was sure all of them were made at the same time. There was no sign of a struggle, but this was only one small patch of dirt. The intruder could have caught up with Justine anywhere in the graveyard.

"Justine!" he shouted again, his initial fear growing incrementally with each silent second.

Instantly, he stilled. Something. He'd heard something… faint, but it sounded like a voice. He waited one second, two…there it was again. Justine's voice. He was certain. It sounded so faint, but not as if it was coming from a distance, which made no sense—

He stared at the front of the crypt and knew without a doubt that she was locked inside. But was she alone? Stepping up close to the front of the structure, he yelled right at the solid granite slab. "Justine, it's Brian. Can you hear me?"

"Yes," her faint voice sounded from inside the crypt.

"Are you all right?"

"Yes, but I can't find a way to open the door from the inside."

Brian scanned the front of the crypt, no clue how to open it from the outside. "How do I open it out here?"

He leaned close to the granite, making sure he understood Justine's instructions before stepping back and looking for the stone key she'd described that opened the door. He retrieved the block from its slot on the column and pressed it into the cleverly crafted lion etching. He hadn't realized he was holding his breath, until it came out in a great whoosh as the granite door slid silently back and Justine tumbled out.

He caught her as her feet got tangled in her rush to get out of the mausoleum, and she clung to him for a moment. With her chest pressed against his, he could feel her rapid heartbeat and couldn't imagine how terrifying it must have been to be trapped inside the crypt.

"Thank you," she said, her voice shaky. She loosened her grip a little and looked up at him, her green eyes finally showing the vulnerability that was buried deep beneath a hard exterior. His breath caught in his throat for just a moment, and before he could change his mind, he lowered his lips to hers.

He knew he wasn't thinking straight, and fully expected her to pull away, but she didn't. She stiffened for just a millisecond, then relaxed in his arms and returned the kiss with the same intensity and passion he saw in her when she was working. Tightening his arms around her, he deepened the kiss, parting her lips with his tongue. Her tongue met his, swirling together in a sensual dance that had his body responding in ways that couldn't be acted on at that moment, in that location.

Suddenly, Justine broke off the kiss and stepped away from him. Her face was flushed and he could see her hardened nipples through her thin T-shirt. She stared at him, her expression a mixture of confusion, desire and fear, and Brian realized that the kiss had surprised her as much as it had him. They'd been so careful around each other, so deliberate, but clearly something much bigger was lurking just beneath the surface.

Something that Justine didn't want anything to do with, if he was reading her correctly.

"I'm sorry," he began.

"No," she stopped him. "Please don't apologize. We were both scared and then relieved. It's a normal reaction."

Brian frowned. He'd been scared and relieved before but hadn't kissed anyone. Still, Justine was clearly shaken enough, so he didn't argue with her. "What happened?"

Justine glanced at the crypt. "I figured out how to open the door and stepped inside to read the inscriptions on the vaults. I heard the footsteps behind me and ran for the door, but it closed before I could get out."

"Did you see him?"

"No. It could have been a man, woman or child, for all I know."

Brian shook his head. "If it was a woman or a child, they were wearing large men's boots. I found a print next to yours. See?" He pointed to the bootprint in front of one of the columns.

Justine stared at the print for a couple of seconds, then nodded.

Brian tried to get a read on her, but she'd slipped back into the guarded state that she usually existed in. His frustration at the entire situation—a situation he'd taken great measures to avoid—took hold, and he felt the blood rise to his face.

"What the hell were you thinking, sneaking out?" he demanded.

Justine's eyes widened and she hesitated before answering. "I didn't want an argument about coming out here."

"We were already out here this morning, looking specifically for a place someone could be hiding. You deliberately lied to me."

"I—I wasn't certain."

Brian shook his head, not buying it for a moment. "And since I didn't see any rope hanging around the library yesterday, I can only assume that you brought one with you, which means you planned to do this before we even arrived at the house today. Stop playing with me, Justine. I'm running out of patience and I do have the authority to remove you from this house."

Justine's expression turned from belligerent to panicked in an instant. "Look, I'm not used to having an audience when I work, much less some hulking male watching my every move. You can't expect me to change the way I feel overnight."

"I don't expect you to change the way you feel at all, but I expect you to change the way you work immediately, because that's what your client—my friends—require."

She studied him for a moment, perhaps looking for a weak point or an opening for her argument, but if that's what she hoped for, she was sorely disappointed. On this issue, Brian had no room for maneuvering.

"Fine," she said, and sighed. "Now that you know what I came out here to find, are you going to give me any grief about searching the graveyard and making a record of what I find?"

"Not in the least. That's your job. My job is protecting

you while you do it. As long as you keep both our jobs in mind, we'll be fine."

Finally, the guilt he'd been waiting to see appeared. "You're right. There's no need to jeopardize your job by doing mine." She dropped her head and stared at the ground.

Brian reached out and placed his hand on her arm. "I'm not worried about jeopardizing my job. I'm worried about jeopardizing your life."

Justine nodded, and when she looked up at him, he caught a glint of unshed tears. "So what now?"

Brian looked around the graveyard until he located a granite marker that was narrow enough to roll. "I guess we figure out if anything interesting is in that crypt." He walked up to the grave marker and pushed it over, then rolled the solid granite piece over and over until it rested across the opening to the crypt.

"Just in case," he said and motioned for Justine to step inside the crypt.

Justine blew out a deep breath, then stepped over the grave marker and into the crypt, Brian right behind.

"Do you think the emeralds are in here?" Brian asked.

"It wouldn't surprise me. The graveyard would be considered hallowed ground. If the voodoo woman used consecrated ground to bind the emeralds and placed them here, the spirits would guard them."

Brian stared. "You mean that's what they would have believed. Not that it would work."

Justine shrugged. "Before I came to laMalediction, I would have absolutely agreed with you."

"But now you don't?"

"Let's just say that now I'm not as closed off to the

possibilities of what may have happened here as I was before."

"Why not?" Brian couldn't help wondering what had caused the shift in Justine's thinking. A spirit hadn't conked Justine on the head or locked her in the crypt.

Justine stared at him for a moment, her brow wrinkled in concentration. "I don't really have the words for it, but it's just a feeling. Something about that house feels alive. It's a very strong sensation and one I've never had before."

"Maybe it's just all the hype combined with the creepiness of the estate and the very real stalker you've acquired."

Justine shook her head. "I don't think so. I understand what you're saying, but what I'm feeling goes so much further than apprehension or fear. It's like I feel something in my soul."

Brian considered her words carefully. He wanted to discount them, but he couldn't force his mind to do so. Overseas, he'd seen things he didn't understand...couldn't explain. Why should he expect everything to have an explanation?

"You feel it, too, don't you?" Justine asked.

"Not like you do. But there's something lying just beneath the surface. Whether it's a man or a spirit, I'd probably get the same feeling."

"But you're not disagreeing."

"No, I'm not. I think it's foolish to ignore what our senses tell us. Foolish, and in some cases deadly." He glanced down the row of vaults. "So, if you were going to hide the emeralds here, I guess you'd put them in the vault?"

"Probably."

He placed his fingers around the edges of one of the

front plates and pulled. It didn't even move an inch. "I don't think we're getting these off of here without a crowbar. There's one in the storage shed at laMalediction. Maybe we should get some supplies and come back."

"You're right," Justine agreed, her expression resigned. "No use putting forth triple effort when the right tools will make it easy. But we can come back today, right?"

"Yeah. I need to find a couple of tools, grab some extra ammunition and give John a call. I want to let him know what we intend to do and give him a check-in time. If he hasn't heard from me by then, I want someone looking for us."

"Good idea." Justine exited the crypt with Brian following behind her.

"Do you think we should close the door?" Justine asked.

"No use that I can see. Whoever followed you out here knew how to operate it, so we're not giving him access he didn't already have." He started across the graveyard to the gate, when something white at the top of the gate caught his eye. Increasing his pace, he approached the gate and realized it was a piece of paper pressed over the top of one of the wrought-iron spikes.

He could see writing on it even before he pulled it off the spike, but the words he saw were the last he expected to see.

Does he know who you are?

He turned to Justine, who had walked up beside him and showed her the note. Her eyes widened as she read the words, but the guarded expression was firmly back in place.

"What does this mean?" he asked her.

"I...I don't know."

Brian studied her face and body language. She wasn't

telling the truth, but what was she leaving out? "The intruder left this for us to find. It must mean something."

"He's a madman. Why does it have to make sense?"

"Even crazy people tell the truth. They just often see it differently than others."

Justine's expression hardened. "What do you want me to say—that I have deep dark secrets? Everyone has secrets, but mine have nothing to do with what's going on here. I told you I don't know what the note means."

She brushed past him and continued down the trail away from the graveyard, never once looking back. Brian stared after her, certain it was high time he found out what Justine was hiding.

Before it got her killed.

THE INTRUDER WATCHED THEM as they left the graveyard. The man found the note, just as intended, and the woman had lied, as expected. Her lie didn't appear to be convincing. The man, her protector, wasn't a fool…he just wasn't in possession of all the facts.

He'd originally thought the woman would leave on her own when she realized someone in Cypriere knew her true identity, but he'd apparently underestimated her. But if the man found out she'd been lying—and to what extent—he might send her away.

Without the woman in residence, there was no job for the man. Then the house would be empty again, and he could finish his work.

Chapter Eleven

Back at laMalediction, Brian instructed Justine to pack some water and food for their return to the graveyard, and headed to the storage shed to find some tools for his new task. As soon as he was inside the shed and out of sight of the main house, he pulled his cell phone from his pocket and gave a mental thanks that he had a signal. He pressed in John's number at the New Orleans Police Department.

"Landry."

"It's Brian."

"Hey, good to hear from you. Is everything all right out in the creepy boondocks?"

"Yes and no." Brian filled John in on all the happenings in Cypriere since the last time they'd talked, but left out the part about Justine sneaking out of the house. He wanted more information before he made a decision on that.

"Wow. That is not how Olivia and I hoped this would go down," John said.

Brian could tell by his voice that John was upset with the news. "Nobody could have expected this," Brian reassured his friend. "It's all disjointed and odd. How could anyone plan for the irrational?"

John sighed. "Hell if I know. The only good thing

GET FREE BOOKS and FREE GIFTS WHEN YOU PLAY THE...
Lucky 7
Just scratch off the silver box with a coin. Then check below to see the gifts you get!
SLOT MACHINE GAME!
YES! I have scratched off the silver box. Please send me the 2 free Harlequin Intrigue® books and 2 free gifts for which I qualify. I understand I am under no obligation to purchase any books, as explained on the back of this card.
❑ I prefer the regular-print edition
182/382 HDL FERM
❑ I prefer the larger-print edition
199/399 HDL FERM
FIRST NAME
LAST NAME
ADDRESS
APT.#
CITY
STATE/PROV.
ZIP/POSTAL CODE
Worth TWO FREE BOOKS plus 2 FREE Mystery Gifts!
Worth TWO FREE BOOKS!
Worth ONE FREE BOOK!
TRY AGAIN!
Visit us at: www.ReaderService.com
H-I-07/11
Offer limited to one per household and not applicable to series that subscriber is currently receiving.
Your Privacy – The Reader Service is committed to protecting your privacy. Our Privacy Policy is available online at www.ReaderService.com or upon request from the Reader Service. We make a portion of our mailing list available to reputable third parties that offer products we believe may interest you. If you prefer that we not exchange your name with third parties, or if you wish to clarify or modify your communication preferences, please visit us at www.ReaderService.com/consumerschoice or write to us at Reader Service Preference Service, P.O. Box 9062, Buffalo, NY 14269. Include your complete name and address.
DETACH AND MAIL CARD TODAY!
© 2011 HARLEQUIN ENTERPRISES LIMITED
Printed in the U.S.A. ® and ™ are trademarks owned and used by the trademark owner and/or its licensee.
H-I-07/11

that came out of my time at laMalediction was meeting Olivia."

"And rescuing Rachel." John's sister had been kidnapped and held hostage in the hidden tunnels below laMalediction by Ross Wheeler, before he'd determined that Olivia was the true heir to the estate.

"Goes without saying, man."

"I need you to do some legwork for me," Brian said.

"Anything you need. Who's the target?"

"Justine Chatry."

John was silent for several seconds before he responded. "Is there something you left out of your story? Something I need to know about the woman you're locked in a house with every night?"

"I can't give you anything concrete, but something doesn't add up. I was watching her face when I showed her the note. She was scared, and then the stone wall immediately went up. She's hiding something. I just need to know if it's relevant to the situation."

"We did a decent background check and she came up clean. You know, if I have to dig any deeper I'm going to have to talk to people."

And any of those people could easily tell Justine the police were checking up on her. The implication of John's statement was clear to Brian, and he'd already weighed the risk involved.

"It's a risk I'll have to take. Something weird is going on here and I don't think it's limited to just laMalediction. The whole town feels off somehow."

"Yeah. I'm not going to lie to you. I'm happy to be gone and I don't ever really want to go back. Driving away from there, it was like a giant weight came off of me."

"Listen to us. We sound like a bunch of scared teens."

"Maybe. Or maybe we just sound like two smart men.

I'm not going to tell you what to do, because I trust your judgment like I do no one else's, but promise me that if you think it's too dangerous for you to handle, you'll get the hell out of there."

"That's a promise I have no problem keeping."

"I'll call you when I have some information."

"Great. Give Olivia a kiss for me." Brian ended the call and slipped the phone back in his pocket, already feeling better. If anyone could dig to the bottom of Justine's lies, it was John. His friend had the uncanny ability to ferret out even the best-hidden secrets. People automatically liked him, and therefore, automatically responded to his questions.

He only hoped that Justine's secret was something of paramount embarrassment and not something more insidious. He liked her, was attracted to her.

Even if he didn't trust her.

JUSTINE PLACED the sandwich fixings on the kitchen counter but didn't make a move for the bread. Instead, she stared out the window over the kitchen sink, trying to control her rising level of panic. She knew exactly what the note meant. After the first two attempts, the stalker knew she wasn't going to leave, so now he was trying to expose her, probably hoping Brian would make her go. She'd lied when Brian had confronted her, hoping to buy more time, but didn't think for a second he'd bought it.

There was no doubt in her mind that Brian would dig deeper into her background. The question was, could she finish her work at laMalediction before he uncovered all the layers of her new, carefully constructed identity? He had all the resources of the New Orleans Police Department at his disposal. How long would it take? One week? A couple of days?

She placed her hands on the counter and leaned forward, trying to remain optimistic about her chances of finishing the job. Worst case, she could beg forgiveness for not telling him the truth because she was ashamed. Anyone would buy that, right?

She blew out a breath. Yeah, people would definitely buy the shame part, but that didn't mean they'd think she should get to continue working at laMalediction. Which meant she had to make tracks quickly. No more leisurely dinners and long nights of sleep. She would bring journals with her to the rental every night and burn the midnight oil.

Another thought crossed her mind and she tried to block it out by reaching for the bread. It was no use. Just the fleeting thought of Brian's lips on hers had her skin tingling all over again, as it had in the swamp. It was so unexpected, she was certain she'd stopped breathing. She'd had the good sense to finally break it off, but she couldn't remember a single step of her entire walk back to laMalediction. Her mind had been fogged with thoughts of Brian…his lips on hers, how his hands would feel on her body.

She shook her head, horrified that she'd started the imagery all over again. This wouldn't do at all. Sure, Brian was an attractive man, but clearly she was just lonely. The last kind of man Justine could allow in her life was a cop. She grabbed the butter knife and started preparing the sandwiches with a vengeance. Who was she kidding? The last kind of man that would want to be involved with *her* was a cop.

If Brian knew the truth, he'd run far, far away.

She finished the sandwiches and secured them in a front pocket of her backpack, then grabbed several bottled waters from the refrigerator and loaded up the inside pocket. At least Brian was willing to allow her to investigate the graveyard, and his suggestion of food meant they wouldn't have to break and return to the house for lunch, which meant less time lost. With any luck, she'd find the answers to some of her questions today.

As she stepped into the entry, Brian walked through the front door. He carried a crowbar and a duffel bag. "I included a hammer, chisel and some other thin tools that we might be able to use in tighter spaces," he said, motioning to the duffel bag. "It's starting to cloud up, so we need to get a move on."

As soon as Justine nodded, Brian exited the house without even so much as a glance at her. Justine secured the pack to her back and followed him out of the house and across the lawn. It was going to be a long afternoon with a cloud of suspicion cast over her, but Justine knew she had to ignore Brian's attitude and focus on getting the answers she needed.

She glanced up as she crossed the yard, still trailing behind Brian. Dark clouds were collecting above the estate, swirling around in various shades of gray. Justine knew it wouldn't be long before the storm developed enough energy to drop down on them. She had to work fast if she was going to discover anything this afternoon.

With the sun tucked behind the clouds, a dark haze had settled over the graveyard, making the light gray granite of the crypts seem to glow in the increasing dimness. Justine shivered slightly and wished she'd brought her jacket, although she knew her momentary chill wasn't due to the weather. Before she could successfully creep herself out, she crossed the graveyard to the main crypt.

"I guess we should have brought a lantern," Justine commented as she peeked inside the dark crypt.

Brian unzipped his bag and pulled out a spotlight. "I've got something better."

Justine nodded. "Where do you want to start?"

"That's a question you should be answering. I mean, I assumed you wanted to open the vaults. I'm hoping you don't want to open any caskets."

"No! I'm hoping it doesn't come to that, but something could be hidden inside the vault along with the caskets." She pulled a piece of folded paper from her pocket. "First, let me take a quick inventory. I made a list of all the Borque family members that I think died at laMalediction."

Brian turned on the spotlight and shined it on the ceiling of the mausoleum from the doorway. The light reflected off the ceiling and illuminated the inside. Justine stepped inside and began comparing the names on her list to the names etched on the individual vaults, checking the names off her list with a pencil as she went. When she got to the last vault, only two names remained on her list. She marked off the name on the last vault and stared at the one remaining name, surprised.

"What's wrong?" Brian asked.

"I don't understand..."

Justine scanned the vaults again to ensure she hadn't made a mistake, but the one name left on her list wasn't contained on any of the etchings.

"Is someone missing?" Brian asked.

"You could say that." She looked up at Brian, still trying to process what this could possibly mean. "There's no vault for Franklin Borque."

Brian's eyes widened. "You're sure?"

Justine nodded. "That's why I double-checked."

"But why would that be? Franklin Borque had to have commissioned the building of this graveyard along with everything else. Why wouldn't he be buried in his own family crypt?"

Justine considered the situation for a moment. "Maybe because of what he did. With his wife dead, Franklin's father probably would have made the decision on his burial place."

"So Franklin may have caused the family too much embarrassment to be allowed to rest in the family crypt?"

"Maybe. Or maybe his father brought him back to New Orleans to rest in a family crypt there."

Brian frowned. "So, if he was buried here, where would the body be?"

"Probably in the graveyard outside of the family mausoleum. If Franklin's family was Christian, they may have insisted he be buried in an unmarked grave outside of the graveyard to punish him for his sins."

"Wow. Excommunicated even in death." Brian looked down the row of vaults. "So what now?"

Justine pointed to a vault that stood as high as her waist and had more elaborate etching than those around it. "We start with Marilyn Borque. If the emeralds are hidden in a vault, it will probably be hers."

Brian passed Justine the spotlight and grabbed his crowbar. "Marilyn it is."

Justine stepped to the side to give him clear access to the vault. She tried not to notice how good his hard body felt as it brushed her in passing. *Focus on the job,* she reminded herself. Brian hesitated in front of the vault and Justine had the fleeting idea that disturbing the dead might be creeping him out, but then she noticed his gaze was concentrated on one corner of the vault.

"What's wrong?" she asked.

"Someone's already been in here."

Brian pointed to a corner of the vault facing and Justine

stepped in for a closer look. Sure enough, around the edge were the telltale scratches in the granite that told her someone had been there before them.

"Can you tell if they were able to open it?" she asked.

"No. I guess we'll just have to see what's inside."

Brian worked the edge of the crowbar under the lip of the vault facing and pushed the bar backward, slowly inching the vault facing from its slot. When he'd worked it out about a half an inch, he removed the crowbar and placed it on the other side of the facing, repeating the process.

"Should I hold the facing so it doesn't fall?" Justine asked.

"No, it's too heavy. I don't want you to hurt yourself. The facing probably won't break hitting the dirt floor, and if it does, I don't really care."

Justine couldn't exactly argue with his logic. Her feet would be in a lot more danger than the facing or the ground. She bit her lower lip as the facing inched out of the granite wall. What would she find inside? She didn't really expect finding the emeralds to be this easy. Surely, the estate attorney, Wheeler, had known of the graveyard and thought to look here already, which probably explained the scratches on the vault facing. But with any luck, there might be more clues contained inside. Something that put her on the right path.

"It's coming loose," Brian said as the facing broke free of the granite wall and fell to the ground.

Justine stepped over the facing and shined the spotlight inside the vault. The ornate gold trimmings on Marilyn Borque's casket created a glare, and she directed the spotlight to one of the walls inside the vault.

"It doesn't look like anything's in here but the casket." She looked over at Brian. "I know I said we're not opening it, but do you think we could pull it out a little? I'd like to look at the scrollwork on the edges."

Brian nodded and grabbed one side of the casket while she wrapped her fingers around the top and bottom of the other side. "Okay," she said, "pull."

They slowly inched the casket out of the vault until a good three feet of it was exposed. Afraid it might drop if they moved it any farther, Justine motioned to Brian to stop and she began to study the gold scrollwork on the sides of the casket.

"Fancy," Brian said. "I figured given the situation, the family would have just thrown her in a pine box."

"If it had been left up to Franklin's family, they probably would have. But remember, Marilyn came from money herself. Her dad traded her in marriage to seal a business deal with Franklin's father. Given that Franklin killed his only daughter, I imagine the Borques were willing to do whatever he asked."

"And you think that the family would have hidden something in or on the casket?"

Justine lifted the spotlight and shined it directly on a piece of scrolling at the corner of the casket. "Not the family. One of the passages in the journal said that Sissy's cousin was going to have the emeralds bound in metal before they hid them. She would only have trusted a family member to do such a thing, which means there was a metalworker close by. He may have also done the scrolling for this casket."

"Makes sense. Do you see anything?"

"Maybe." Justine ran her finger over a section of the scrolling, then tilted her head to the side. She could feel her heart beat a bit faster when she recognized the lion worked sideways into the scrolling. A quick inspection of the other side revealed no sign of the lion, although no one would ever have noticed the scrolling was different unless they'd been inspecting every inch. The work was absolutely incredible.

"Hold this a minute," she said and passed the spotlight to Brian.

Brian stepped near her and shined the spotlight at the end of the casket where she'd been working. "What is it?"

"The lion. Worked into the scrolling on this end." She pressed her fingers into the lion scrolling, searching for something that moved, but found nothing. She studied the scrolling again and realized that the section with the lion sat a tiny bit higher than the scrolling beneath it. Placing her fingers on both sides of the lion, she pushed the entire piece of scrolling down about an inch.

A drawer at the bottom of the casket popped open.

"Are the emeralds there?" Brian asked as he inched past the end of the casket for a better look at the drawer.

"No," Justine said as she pulled a small stack of yellow paper out of the drawer, feeling her pulse increase when she realized what she held. "It's the missing pages from the journals."

"Missing pages?"

"Yeah. I noticed yesterday that some of the pages had been torn out of the journals."

"You think they will tell you where the emeralds are hidden?"

"That's what I'm hoping." And what happened to Marilyn's child. Justine tried to control her excitement. It may still mean nothing. Just because she hadn't found a vault for Marilyn's child didn't mean he had survived. If Franklin had killed the child, he probably would have insisted he be buried with the servants.

"I need to grab my backpack," she said, and stepped

out of the crypt to retrieve her pack, which lay next to the opening. She pulled a plastic container from the main pocket and placed the pages inside.

"You came prepared, I see," Brian commented, pointing at her container.

"When you work with old documents all the time, you learn to carry the right storage containers." She closed the container and slipped it back in her backpack. As she zipped her pack, thunder boomed overhead, making her jump.

Brian hurried out of the crypt and they both stared up at the swirling sky. "I should have known better," Brian said. "We need to get back to the house before the bottom drops out."

"The casket?" Justine asked.

Brian stepped back inside the crypt. "Let's just slide it back into place. We can deal with the vault facing later."

Justine stepped in behind him and closed the drawer at the bottom of the casket. The lion in the etching slid automatically back into place. She nodded to Brian and they slowly pushed the casket back into the slot. When they lacked about an inch of getting the casket inside the vault, it seemed to hang.

"Hold on a second," Brian said and stooped to look underneath the casket. "There's a screw that's sticking out of the bottom just a bit. It's catching on the wall. We'll have to lift it a little to get it over."

Justine changed her grip on the casket to get a better hold on it for lifting, but Brian didn't rise from the floor. "Is something wrong?" she asked.

"The wall right below the vault. It looks strange."

"Strange how?" She heard an audible click.

"Strange in that a piece of it moves."

As Brian rose from the floor, Justine watched in amazement as the back wall of the crypt slid open. She gasped and Brian turned around, following her gaze. Brian stepped up to the opening and looked inside.

"There's a stone stairwell in here."

Justine stepped behind him and peeked into the dark space. It was a good three feet wide and contained a set of stone stairs that pitched straight down into inky blackness. Justine reached behind her and grabbed the spotlight and passed it to Brian.

"Can you see anything?" she asked, as he shined the light down the stairwell.

"About fifteen feet down is the bottom. Looks like the walls and floor are also made of stone."

"I don't get it. I've never heard of a cellar in a crypt."

Brian shook his head. "I don't think it's a cellar. I can't make it out completely, but it looks like there's a tunnel at the end of the stairs to the right."

"Do you think it could run all the way to the main house?"

As Brian looked back at Justine a huge roll of thunder boomed overhead. "Anything's possible, but there's no time to check it out now. That storm moved in early. We've got to get out of here before we're trapped at laMalediction."

"What about the casket?"

"It's far enough in that it's not going anywhere." Brian pressed the lever below the casket and the door at the back of the crypt slid back into place. He gathered his tools and stuffed them inside his duffel bag, then rolled the grave marker out of the way of the main crypt door. Justine tripped the lever as soon as the doorway was clear, then slung her backpack over her shoulder and hurried out of the graveyard with Brian.

She couldn't wait to review the journal pages, but hoped they made it out of laMalediction before the storm hit. If there was a tunnel in the crypt that led to laMalediction, they were sitting ducks until they closed the entry point into the house.

Chapter Twelve

Justine stood at the living-room window of the rental house and peered outside, watching the rain pour from the sky. They'd barely made it back to the rental before the bottom dropped out of the sky. For the past fifteen minutes, rain had fallen in sheets so thick you couldn't see more than a foot or so beyond the window, and it showed no sign of slowing.

Brian hadn't said another word about her sneaking out of the house. In fact, he hadn't spoken at all on the drive from the estate, and he'd headed straight for the shower when they arrived at the rental. She knew he was probably worried about the tunnel and what it might mean if there was an entrance to laMalediction that he and John had not located. That fancy security system on the doors and windows wouldn't keep anyone out if they had a way in from below. Brian and John had boarded up the basement entry to the tunnels, but the tunnel in the graveyard might provide hidden access into the house that didn't connect through the basement.

Justine let the drape fall back across the window and stepped over to the dining table. The power was on for now, but she didn't figure it would last much longer in the storm. At least her laptop was fully charged and she had a lantern that would provide her light all night, if her research occupied that much time. The container with the missing diary pages sat on the dining table, and Justine had started to hunker down and read the documents several times now, but every time she started to slide into the dining chair, she'd felt compelled to peek out the living-room window.

Someone was watching.

She knew it as surely as she knew her own name. Nothing was visible in the storm, and with all the drapes drawn, no one could see inside the rental house, but Justine knew he was out there. Watching. Waiting.

What did he want from her? It seemed it was her very presence in Cypriere that he resented. So why was she such a threat? Was he hoping to find the emeralds before she did? And how many people were aware of the story or her real reason for being there? The story of the emeralds may not have been in the newspapers, but some of the locals probably knew the tales.

The attorney, Wheeler, had probably heard about the emeralds from the previous estate attorney or from the old caretaker, Aubrey. Aubrey had lived on the estate since he was a little boy, and retired after being held hostage by Wheeler when Olivia occupied the house. But if Wheeler had left no indication of a partner, Justine could only assume someone else was working alone.

Regardless, it was clear that someone wanted her out of Cypriere. The notes and attack had been directed at her. Even slashing the tires on Brian's Jeep could still have been done just to prevent her from getting to laMalediction. That made sense, of course, because if she wasn't in residence, Brian wouldn't need to be, either. By forcing Justine to leave, the intruder got an empty estate. But Justine felt as if there was more to it than that.

Based on the notes he'd left, the intruder knew Justine's

real past. Did he also know what she was searching for—proof that she was a descendant of Marilyn Borque? If so, that might better explain things. If the intruder suspected she was a descendant of Marilyn Borque, he might think she had inside information, or intuition, that would allow Justine to locate the emeralds before he could.

Justine flopped into the dining chair and opened the plastic container. What she needed to do was stop guessing what was going on and do her job. She pulled the stack of diary entries out and placed them in front of her. The first entry she recognized as Marilyn's handwriting.

April 28, 1863
Sissy took my child to her cousin late last night, when the master couldn't see her go. She'll be back before morning. I don't think Franklin will look for my child. I think he just wants him out of his sight. Wants any reminder of my lover wiped away. Sissy's cousin will take the child to her family in New Orleans who will care for him. I've given him his father's name, Dubois. I will light a candle for his safe passage and pray to the Gods that his life is full and happy, the way his father would have wanted.

Justine's spirits dropped when she finished the passage. She was happy Marilyn's child had made it safely away from laMalediction, but in researching her lineage, she had not come across a single Dubois. Could she have been wrong all this time? When Justine's mother had told her the stories when she was a child, she'd described things so well—the house isolated in the swamp with secret tunnels, the mean husband who became obsessed with cursed emeralds and the ghost that continued to haunt the estate, bound to the grounds until the curse was lifted by a descendant of the Borques.

Her mother had been healthy when she'd told Justine that story. Of that, she was certain. The first time Justine had ever seen her mother break from reality, she was only eight years old, but even then it was clear to her that something was wrong. But the mother who'd told her the story about the bad man and the emeralds wasn't the sick mother. She knew what sick looked like.

When Olivia had first come to her with the story, almost apologetic at what she considered a bizarre request, Justine had worked to not appear overeager. How many cursed emeralds could there possibly be hidden away in the swamp? This was Justine's golden opportunity to fit the missing pieces of her mother's medical history into place. If Justine could prove that Marilyn Borque and her descendants weren't mentally ill, then Justine might let down the wall she'd carefully erected around herself. Might allow herself to form a relationship that went deeper than acquaintance level, without the fear that something bad might happen to anyone close to her.

Someone like Brian.

She clamped her mind down on that thought before it could even fully develop. Even if she was free to form relationships, the last place she'd start was with a cop. And not just any cop, but the nephew of the man who'd arrested her mother. The man who'd hauled her mother away, screaming and scratching, and held her in a cell without calling for medical care.

The man who'd beaten her during the arrest and almost killed her with his neglect.

"Find anything?" Brian's voice sounded from the living room.

He stood at the edge of the tiny dining area, drying his

short hair with a towel. He wore a pair of sweatpants and his T-shirt was slung over his shoulder. Muscles rippled across his abdomen, chest and arms, and his tanned skin looked as if it wasn't quite dry.

"Justine?" His voice broke into her lustful thoughts and she diverted her gaze upward to his face, embarrassed to realize that she'd been so busy admiring his body that she hadn't answered the question.

"Sorry," she said and dropped her gaze down to the table, but not before she caught a hint of a smile from Brian. Great. He'd noticed her major faux pas. "I just got started, but the first page indicates that the child was sent to live with some of Sissy's family in New Orleans."

"That's good," Brian said. "I was sorta worried…"

"Me, too," she said, her appreciation for Brian rising a bit more for his concern over a child from long ago. "I was afraid I might find something I didn't want to in that graveyard."

"Knowing what we do about Franklin Borque, it definitely crossed my mind more than once. Any mention of Marilyn's lover?"

Justine felt the heat rise up her face just a tiny bit at the word *lover,* but she didn't miss a beat this time in replying. "Nothing yet. It's weird."

Brian slid into a chair across the table from her. "What is?"

"Well, a journal is the most logical place to find a woman's musings on her lover, but aside from the couple we're already aware of, Marilyn doesn't mention him much at all."

"Maybe you'll find something in the missing pages."

Justine shook her head. "I don't think so. In the diary that covered the span when Marilyn sent for her lover until the time Franklin returned home, I only saw a couple of places where pages could be missing."

Brian frowned. "So why wouldn't she talk about him? It sounded like he was her great love. He traveled to see her despite the remote location and her being married to a powerful man. He fathered a child with her, but then didn't stick around to see him born, or to raise him?"

"Exactly my point. It doesn't make sense. If Marilyn had sent the child to live with his father, that would have made sense, but it's almost as if he vanished from her life."

"Maybe he did. Maybe he died."

Justine stared at him. Her first inclination was to argue, but she knew that was her romantic side thinking, not her practical one. Her practical side had known when she first read the diaries that something was amiss. She just hadn't wanted to face that possibility until she knew for sure.

She sighed and Brian gave her a sympathetic look. "You already thought of that, didn't you?"

"Yeah. I was just hoping it wasn't the case. I mean, the woman already had so much tragedy in her life. It's just sad."

Brian nodded. "And she can't even get any rest in death with us and whoever else disturbing her vault."

"Do you think it was Wheeler who opened the vault?"

"Possibly. He was desperate to find the emeralds and I imagine he knew enough of the old lore to think along some of the same lines you have."

"I don't get it though. I mean, I assumed he wanted the emeralds to sell them. The newspapers reported how he'd embezzled millions from his clients over the years and the house of cards was about to tumble, but without the history attached to the stones, I don't think they'd be worth millions of dollars. A collector might pay it with the story attached, but then Wheeler would have had to out himself."

Brian shifted his gaze from Justine to the floor and frowned.

"What?" Justine asked. "You know something. What is it you're not telling me?"

Brian looked back up and stared at her for a couple of seconds, his indecision clear. "If I tell you the rest of the story, you have to promise it will not leave this house. Given all the things that have happened, I don't think it's fair for you not to have all the facts about the situation with Wheeler. You may even change your mind about staying."

Justine's pulse quickened. If Brian thought she'd leave over what he was about to say, it must be big.

"Wheeler wasn't after the emeralds for their value alone but because of the way the estate documents are written. It's complicated, but the gist of it is that until the emeralds are found, the estate can't be sold. The land that makes up the estate is full of oil. Wheeler had the surveys done."

"And his attorney's cut from selling would have amounted to millions? That doesn't sound right."

"As an attorney, he wouldn't have made millions, but as an heir he stood to make a killing, literally."

Justine's mind reeled. "An heir? You're kidding me. How…?"

"Apparently Franklin Borque had a mistress, the person *he* would have been with if his father hadn't made him marry Marilyn for the business deal. That mistress had a child who had a child and that line leads straight to Wheeler. The police found the documentation in his office to prove it all."

Justine struggled to remain calm. "Do you have access to the documentation?"

"I could probably get it, but how would that help you?"

Justine's mind raced to come up with a plausible reason that she'd need the information for her research on the emeralds. "I wondered if there was anyone else from that family line in Cypriere. If so, he could be behind the problems at laMalediction."

Brian frowned. "According to his research, Wheeler was the only living relative left from that family line, but that was never verified. I suppose if there were others, he'd hardly have been handing out that information and a big cut of his inheritance. You'd think if someone in Cypriere was descended from Franklin Borque they would have already been yelling for their share of the estate."

"Not if they're behind all the stuff happening. Take Tom Breaux for instance. He is so entrenched in the old tales of voodoo and haunts that I'd bet he wouldn't set foot on the estate grounds or take a dime of money from the sale. He thinks Olivia stirred something up by coming here. Not intentionally, of course, but I'd bet he's not the only one who feels that way."

"Or he could be a very convincing actor and is trying to scare you off." Brian sighed. "Olivia thought laMalediction was just another job. When Wheeler accused her of being a descendant of Marilyn Borque, she was as shocked as anyone else."

"Did she ever find any proof?"

"No, but Wheeler seemed certain, and Olivia is a dead ringer, if you'll pardon the expression, for Marilyn Borque. I suppose when it comes down to settling the estate, she can have a DNA test to prove her relationship."

"The graveyard," Justine said, realizing how important that discovery had been, and not just for her own work.

"It will probably come in handy. I'll call John after supper and get him to email you the documents found at Wheeler's office since I don't have a computer here."

"That's great. I can print everything, and we can compare it to what we know about the locals."

Brian rose from his chair. "I don't want to start cooking anything, given the weather. I'm afraid I might not get to finish. I figured I'd make a sub sandwich for supper. You want one?"

"Sure. Thanks."

Justine watched as Brian removed food from the refrigerator and started assembling the subs. She opened her laptop, at least trying to look as if she was working, but the emeralds were the last thing on her mind.

The information Brian had given her changed everything—opened up a whole other avenue of research for her family tree. And one she wasn't pleased about pursuing at all. Based on what she knew about Wheeler, the man had been stark-raving mad, and after reading the diaries, she had no doubt about Franklin Borques's mental health.

She crossed her arms in front of her chest, trying to block out the cold chill that passed over her. Heaven help her, if her mother was descended from Franklin and not Marilyn, Justine's search for a normal life was over.

BRIAN SLIPPED INTO his bedroom after dinner and closed the door behind him. He retrieved his cell phone from the top of the dresser and was relieved to see that he still had service despite the storm. It wasn't quite five o'clock yet and he was hoping to catch John before he left the police station.

"Landry," John answered on the first ring.

"Hey, it's Brian. I was afraid I wouldn't catch you there."

"I got held up with paperwork on a B and E, but as soon as we stop talking, I am on the way to dinner with Olivia."

"Sounds nice," Brian said, and although he was genuinely happy for his friend, he felt a tinge of jealousy. Not of Olivia, but of her and John's relationship. Something he wasn't likely to ever find.

"Well, she's cooking, which isn't always nice, but it's never uninteresting." John laughed. "So what's up?"

Brian filled John in on their discoveries in the graveyard.

"Wow," John said. "And you think the tunnel from the graveyard might lead to the house?"

"I can't see any other reason for it. We didn't have time to check it out today, but you can bet it's first on my list as soon as this storm breaks."

"If that tunnel enters the house somewhere other than the basement, it goes a long way to explaining a lot of things."

"I agree," Brian said. "What about that other thing I asked you to check on?"

"Sorry, man. I haven't had a chance to do more than the cursory stuff, and it's all clear. I'll dig deeper first thing in the morning, and get with you as soon as I have something."

"Sounds good." Brian paused for a couple of seconds, then finally told his friend what he'd been hesitant to say. "I told Justine about Wheeler's relation to Borque. I know you don't want the facts to get out, but I thought she had a right to know everything about the situation she's in—in case she decided it wasn't worth the risk."

John was silent for a bit, and Brian was afraid he'd

angered his friend, but finally he spoke. "I agree, given the things that have happened since she's been there, it's wrong to withhold the information. But, Brian, you're asking me to dig into her background, which tells me there's something about her that doesn't sit right with you. Are you sure it was safe to give her that information?"

"You're right. It's a bit of duplicity. I think she's hiding something, but at the same time, I don't think she'll leak the information."

"I've always trusted your read on people and I'm not about to stop now. Just make sure this woman isn't clouding your judgment. I met her in New Orleans with Olivia. She's not exactly hard on the eyes and she's sharp. A lesser man than you might be swayed by a couple of her attributes."

A vivid image of Justine's never-ending legs flashed through his mind and he shifted uncomfortably in his sweats. "I haven't failed to notice her attributes, but this is business. She also pointed out that if Wheeler was a Borque, then others in Cypriere may be, too. For all we know, someone could have been in on the whole thing with Wheeler."

"At this point, anything is possible. I'll scan all the documents tomorrow, and email copies."

"Great," Brian said, and gave his friend Justine's email address. "Thanks, John."

"No problem. And, Brian—watch your back."

"Always."

Chapter Thirteen

It was almost eleven o'clock when Justine finally hopped in the shower for a quick pass, not wanting to linger with the storm raging. The lightning had ceased for the moment, but based on the news reports, the storm system had no intention of releasing Cypriere from its grip for another twenty-four hours. If that held true, there was no way they'd be able to reach laMalediction the next morning. The roads would be impassable, and even if Brian's Jeep could manage it, he was far too cautious to even try.

Being closed up all evening in the tiny rental house with Brian had been hard, especially with her emotions all over the place. The information about Wheeler had sent her reeling, and she was barely able to keep the stress from showing on her face and in her voice. Every conversation required a concentrated effort for her to maintain a semblance of control. Even during the short amount of time they'd taken to eat the sandwiches Brian had prepared, the conversation had seemed stilted.

She knew the dark cloud hanging over her head was causing her to be less focused on the now, less normal in normal conversation, but even Brian had seemed distracted. She wondered briefly if her sneaking out was still bothering him or the tunnel, or if it was something else entirely. The fact that she had no earthly idea how to read him was a stark reminder that she didn't really know anything about the man she was sharing space with, other than the surface-level things. Given how many secrets she held below the surface, she knew Brian might have his own.

She ran a comb through her wet hair and sighed, wishing for the first time in her life that she'd paid attention when her mother was trying to teach her the old ways, especially when she was working on "relaxation" potions. Justine could have used one right now.

She slipped on yoga pants and a T-shirt and pulled her wet hair into a ponytail to dry. What she needed was that paperwork from Wheeler's office, and fast, before she worked herself into a heart attack.

Brian had already said his good-nights before her shower, and she noticed the door to his bedroom was closed as she left the bathroom and walked the short distance down the hall to her bedroom, the lamp from the living room illuminating the hallway just enough to see. She'd left the lamp on in her bedroom and clicked it off just before sliding into bed.

The sheets were cool and she shivered for just a second before they began to warm to her body. *That's what I get for going to bed with wet hair. I'll end up with a cold and have no one to blame but myself.*

She turned on her side and listened to the sounds of the storm outside. The thunder and lightning was starting again, first at a distance, but creeping closer with every passing minute. For the first time ever, she wished she had a television she could turn on to block out the sound of the storm. Justine almost never watched television, much happier to sit down with a good book. In the past, a rainy day had seemed the perfect setting for curling up with a book and a cup of hot chocolate.

But now the storm seemed almost ominous. As if with

every pass, it brought things to the surface in Cypriere. Things that used to be at rest. A practical person would call her fanciful for thinking such things. Her mother would swear she was a medium. Somewhere in the middle might lie the truth.

Closing her eyes, she tried to blank her mind and relax. *Think of something else. Something pleasant and warm and sunny.* Turning her imagination to the tropical vacation she was saving for, she began to drift off to sleep.

The sound of glass breaking and a hard object hitting her square in the back made her bolt upright in the bed. Not even a second later, the house alarm sounded. Before she could even register what had happened, her bedroom door burst open and Brian ran in, gun drawn.

"Get down!" he yelled as he pulled the drapes to the side and peeked out the window.

Justine slid out of the bed and onto the floor, reaching back with one hand to try and find the object that had hit her in the back. Her hand hit something wet and hard and she pulled it off the bed, trying to make out what it was with the little bit of light streaming into the bedroom from the living-room lamp.

It was a rock with a piece of paper wrapped around it, dripping wet from the storm.

"Do you see anyone?" she asked, barely able to see Brian as he peered out the window.

"No. I'm sure the coward left as soon as he dispatched whatever he put through the window. Did it hit you?"

"Yeah, in my back, but I'm okay. It startled me more than anything."

Brian walked into the hall and disarmed the alarm, then reentered the bedroom and sat on the bed. She rose from the floor and handed him the rock. "I guess it's pointless to try and get fingerprints."

"Probably." He removed the rubber band that held the paper in place and peeled the paper off the rock. The ink was blurred from the rain, but Justine could easily see what was written.

Have you told him?

It took every ounce of strength for Justine to stifle the cry that wanted to escape. She looked at the note, taking a moment to gather herself before she faced Brian.

"This has to mean something," Brian said.

"He's a madman. It doesn't have to mean anything."

Brian's eyes locked with her. "You don't believe that. Your eyes give you away. What are you hiding from me, Justine?"

"Nothing!" Justine jumped up from the bed and stared down at Brian. "I've told you everything I know about this place—the journals, the emeralds. The graveyard was the only thing I hid, and I've already told you why."

Brian shook his head. "He knows I'm aware of the graveyard. There's something else he thinks you haven't told me."

Justine blew out a breath. "Well, if I haven't told you, then it's something I don't know yet, either. Maybe he thinks I've made more progress with my research than I have. Maybe he thinks I'm stirring up a ghost. Whatever it is, I don't know."

"Okay." Brian rose from the bed, still holding the rock and the note. "Maybe you're right. Maybe he thinks you know something that you don't, but obviously he's not going away. If you're keeping something from me, no matter how small or how insignificant you think it may be, I need to know."

Justine stared at the floor for a moment, then looked him directly in the eyes. "I have not shared every intimate detail of my life with you, and I won't. But I am not keeping information from you that's relevant to my work here."

Brian's eyes locked on hers, unwavering. She held his gaze, determined not to look away. She wasn't lying. Her search for her own past had nothing to do with the missing emeralds she was hired to find. If she was guilty of anything, it was omission, but she didn't care. Clearly, she was the intruder's target, not Brian.

Finally, he gave her a single nod, but Justine didn't believe for a minute that she'd convinced him. He was giving her the benefit of the doubt because he was a gentleman, but that benefit wouldn't likely extend much further. If he wasn't already picking her carefully created identity apart, he would be soon.

"I'll tape a plastic bag over the hole to keep the rain out," he said finally. "That will hold it until I can manage something better, as I'm sure the landlord will blame us for the damage and be in no hurry to repair it properly."

"Will the alarm system still work?"

"Yeah. It was the sound of the glass breaking that set it off, but there's nothing to stop me from arming the system again." He inclined his head toward his room. "Why don't you take my room. I'll stay in here until the window is repaired."

Justine nodded and walked silently down the hall into Brian's room. She slipped into the bed and turned off the lamp burning on the nightstand. There was no light from the outside because of the storm, so the room was pitch-black. Justine didn't particularly like it, but she was afraid her silhouette would show if she left the light on. That someone might be standing out in the storm watching.

She slid down between the sheets and pulled the covers up close to her face. The smell of Brian's aftershave lingered on the sheets, the scent masculine and arousing. The masculine part was comforting. When it came to sheer force and instinct, Justine couldn't think of anyone she'd rather have protecting her than Brian. But as she drifted off into a light slumber, with Brian's scent wrapped around her, she realized her biggest worry wasn't the stalker, or even Brian finding out her past.

It was the way Brian made her feel.

JUSTINE AWAKENED the next morning with a start at her unfamiliar surroundings. It took her a second to remember the events of the night before and that she was in Brian's bed. She slid out of the warmth of the covers and checked her watch. Seven o'clock. Given the excitement of last night and her two thousand worries, she was surprised she'd slept at all, much less to a time she'd consider "late" on a normal day.

She didn't even have to look out the window to know it was still raining, but she pulled the heavy drape to the side and looked out at the gray sheets of water anyway. The timing couldn't have been worse. The missing diary pages were beginning to fill in the blanks to her many unanswered questions, and she was only halfway through them, but she still thought the graveyard held more answers.

And quite possibly, a tunnel into laMalediction.

What a discovery that would be. It would prove that someone made of flesh and blood was haunting the house, and not a ghost. And maybe, just maybe, she'd find the emeralds somewhere out there in the swamp. The graveyard was consecrated ground, and it appeared as if Franklin Borque had not been interred there. It would make sense for Sissy's cousin to secure the stones somewhere she knew Franklin's spirit couldn't go.

Sighing, she dropped the drape back in place and left the bedroom. Whatever may lie in the graveyard waiting to be discovered, it wasn't going to happen today. No way would Brian risk traveling to laMalediction in this storm, especially when it showed no signs of lessening.

The smell of coffee hit her as soon as she stepped into the hall, and she entered the living room with a bit of trepidation at having to face Brian in the cold, gray light of day. He stood at the kitchen counter, pouring a cup of the steaming coffee, and looked back at her when the living-room floor creaked.

"Coffee?" he asked.

"I would love some," she said, and slipped onto a stool at the bar that separated the kitchen from the tiny dining room.

Brian poured another cup and slid it in front of her, along with a container of sugar and sweetener packets.

"Thanks," she said, and occupied herself with adding sweetener to the coffee.

"I guess I don't have to tell you that today's a bust. This storm is supposed to continue until evening."

"Since it's been coming down like that all night, I kinda figured." She took a sip of her coffee and tried to sound normal as she delivered her next statement. "Unless you need me for anything around here, I thought I'd drive into New Orleans. There's a couple of things I'd like to check up on."

Brian looked across the counter at her and nodded. "Did you find a lead in the diary pages?"

"I'm not sure. Their thinking is so different than mine that I'm afraid I might miss something important. I want to talk to a woman I know about some of the old ways."

"A voodoo woman?"

"A priestess, actually."

Brian raised his eyebrows. "I thought you didn't believe in the old ways?"

"I don't hold much stock in them, but Marilyn Borque did. I want a second opinion on how the emeralds would have been bound. I won't reveal the actual situation or the location, of course."

"No, of course not. Well, if it helps you decipher the past, I'm all for it."

Justine's shoulders relaxed and she realized how tense she'd been. "What will you do?"

"Get a better patch job on the window and see about getting a new one. Maybe visit our friends at the café and see if I can learn anything more about the locals. I think someone in Cypriere is behind the things happening. I'm going to have John start running some background checks on a few of them—maybe help me come up with a motive."

"Did you ask John about the paperwork from Wheeler's office?"

"Yeah. He's supposed to scan the documents first thing this morning, and email them all to you."

"Great. Maybe if I finish up early with the priestess, I can swing by the library and do a little research based on Wheeler's documents. I may be able to find a starting point with some surnames...help narrow down your list of suspects for John to check on."

"I appreciate anything you're able to find, but don't let it distract you from your real work. I can handle the protection duty." He looked a little embarrassed. "I know it doesn't seem like it, given that you're been attacked twice on my watch—"

Justine waved her hand to cut him off. "I don't think anything like that. You can't prepare for everything that can happen. No one could have known that we'd run into so much adversity from the very first day."

"No," Brian agreed, although he still didn't appear

overly convinced. "But that first attack should have put us on high alert. I think we've both been lax about our safety."

"If someone wanted me dead," Justine argued, "I already would be. You know that. I think he's just trying to scare me."

"For now. But if he doesn't succeed…"

"I'll just have to work faster. Maybe the priestess will be able to give me more direction—save me some time." She rose from the stool, still clutching her coffee. "I better get ready and get on the road. I figure the drive may take a while, with the storm."

Brian nodded. "I'm going to pay a visit to the café. Drive safe."

"Count on it." Justine left the kitchen and headed into her bedroom. She glanced at the window and saw the plastic peeking out from behind the drapes. She pulled on a pair of jeans, a long-sleeve T-shirt and her tennis shoes, then grabbed her car keys.

Brian was already gone when she left the rental house. As she drove down the narrow road, she hoped that the information from Wheeler's office gave her the answers she sought, but at the same time she was afraid it wouldn't be the answers she wanted.

THE CAFÉ WAS about half-full when Brian stepped inside. No surprise, really, given the weather. A lot of people were probably taking a weather-related holiday. He slipped onto a stool at the bar next to Chris Pauley, the guy who'd taken care of his tire problem. Chris didn't even look up as he took his seat, but Tom, the café owner, nodded briefly before turning back to the grill.

"You still here, city boy?" Chris said, still looking down at his coffee. "I would have thought those slashed tires would be an indication that you weren't wanted around here."

"It was an indication, all right. I just don't care."

Chris looked up at Brian, an amused expression on his face. "Guess you got more money than sense, then."

"I'm here on business. The estate pays all my expenses, so I couldn't care less about the cost."

"That right? Well, then, I'll order some more tires like what you got, if you planning on sticking around awhile longer. Might see a sharp increase in my business that way."

Brian stared directly at Chris. "Careful, now. Someone might think you're the one behind the problems if you're the one profiting."

Chris leaned back on his stool, his face turning red with anger. "Are you accusing me of something?"

Brian shrugged. "Do I need to be?"

"You better check yourself, mister. You can't come walking into town, swinging your weight around, and accusing decent hardworking people of such things."

"I wasn't aware that I had."

"Well, see that you don't." Chris slid off the stool and tossed a couple of dollars on the counter. As he shoved his wallet in his jean's pocket, he stared at Brian. "You might want to reconsider your current employment. Not everything can be replaced with money."

Chris whirled around and exited the café. The rest of the patrons pretended to be busy with their food and coffee, but Brian knew not a single one of them had missed a word of the exchange.

Tom plated the food from the grill and passed the plates to Deedee, who scurried away, careful not to make eye contact with Brian. "You want coffee?" Tom asked.

"Yes, please, and I'll order breakfast here in a bit. I'm not quite ready to eat yet."

Tom poured a cup of coffee and leaned against the counter. "You got Chris pretty riled up."

Brian took a sip of the steaming liquid, then looked directly at Tom. "Really? Sounded like *he* was threatening *me*. Not the other way around."

"Well now, you might have hit on a sore spot with ol' Chris. You ain't the first person that's accused him of breaking something so he could charge to fix it."

"Sounds like a real nice guy. I'm sorry I pissed him off."

Tom laughed. "I can tell you're really tore up about it. Chris is all right for the most part. He's just a little rough around the edges and a bit of a hothead."

Brian took another sip of coffee, carefully formulating his conversation in his mind. Chris Pauley had set off alarms since their exchange at his garage. If Tom was in a talking mood, Brian might be able to get information out of him as long as he didn't ask the wrong thing.

"What's he got to be so angry about?" Brian asked. "This town seems nice, quiet…he's got a good business going, with no competition. He probably fishes and hunts and there's no shortage of that around here. Seems almost perfect for a simple life."

Tom nodded. "You'd be correct, sir. Cypriere is indeed the perfect spot for an outdoorsman looking to live quietly, but Chris always had ideas bigger than that. Wanted to own a car dealership in the city, not some garage in a town with a handful of people. 'Delusions of grandeur' my grandma used to call them."

"Seems like a big stretch," Brian agreed, "from small-town garage to big-city dealership. That would take some serious cash. Does Chris have a millionaire relative with one foot in the grave?"

"Hell, no. His granddaddy built that garage and it's fed their family for three generations. There ain't never been any millionaires in Cypriere except what lived at that hell house you're here to work in." Tom stopped talking suddenly, his brow wrinkled in concentration.

"You know," Tom continued, his voice low, "back when that attorney was causing trouble, I saw Chris coming out from the road to the estate a couple of times. I asked him about it, but he called me a liar. I'm a lot of things, but blind and a liar ain't two of them."

"You think he had some deal with the attorney and that's how he was going to get the money?"

Tom shook his head. "I don't know, but something was going on. Something he didn't want nobody to know, that was clear."

"Does he live close to the estate?"

"Until a month ago, he lived in a room behind the garage. Bought my fishing cabin from me." He frowned. "Paid cash, as a matter of fact. Twenty thousand in cash."

Brian tried to control his excitement. "Was your cabin in Cypriere?"

"Sorta. It's down the bayou, a ways from town. You can only get there by boat. There's no road at all—just the three cabins stuck out there on the bayou. Great fishing. A man could literally live off the fish alone."

"Sounds like something I'll be looking for soon," he said, trying to sound nonchalant. "Nothing fancy. Just something for a little weekend fishing and relaxation. I don't suppose anyone else in that location is interested in selling?"

Tom rubbed his chin with one hand. "There might be—"

The bells above the café door jangled and Brian turned

to see who had caused Tom to stop speaking. Sheriff Blanchard entered and slid onto a stool next to Brian. Tom's gaze cut over to the sheriff and his mood changed completely. He stiffened and his expression became closed off.

"Sheriff," Tom acknowledged and then looked back at Brian. "You interested in breakfast yet?"

"Yeah," Brian said, disappointed that his bout of good information had apparently come to a screeching halt. "I'll have the special, eggs scrambled."

Tom nodded and passed a cup of coffee to Sheriff Blanchard before turning to the grill. Sheriff Blanchard poured packets of sugar in his coffee and stirred. Finally, he took a big sip then looked over at Brian. "Saw you had a bit of trouble at the rental house."

Brian feigned ignorance. "What do you mean?"

"Noticed the tarp on the window when I was making my rounds this morning."

"Yeah. Bad storm last night. Bedroom window started to leak a little."

Sheriff Blanchard narrowed his eyes. "Leaky window, huh? You don't have anything to report to me?"

"I wasn't aware that old caulking was something the sheriff's department looked into."

Sheriff Blanchard's expression hardened. "If the problem was only old caulking then you'd be right, although I got the tools to loan you if you're interested in fixing it. But see, old Ms. Bergeron, who lives next door to the rental, called me this morning and said she heard an alarm going off at the rental house right after the sound of breaking glass."

"Why, Sheriff, you sound concerned, especially for someone that didn't want to believe anything was going on in your town."

"What's going on in this town is you people have stirred up a bunch of bored kids who are making a mess and costing decent people money. Sammy don't have the money to be replacing windows on his rental just because he had the poor judgment to rent to you."

"I'm sure the estate will be happy to pay for any repairs needed to Sammy's property. You needn't worry yourself over his potential loss, especially since it's clear you're not worried about putting a stop to these hooligans you blame for all the problems in this town. One might begin to question the parenting skills of the good people of Cypriere to have produced such monsters."

A blush crept up Sheriff Blanchard's neck and onto his face. "Now see here. This was a quiet, decent town until that writer woman came here stirring things up. The only trouble this town has ever seen has come from that house, and when people let that relic sink into the bayou where it belongs, things will be right again."

"It's just a house, Sheriff. Houses don't throw rocks through windows trying to scare young women. You might want to pass around to those 'kids' that scare tactics only piss Justine off."

Sheriff Blanchard gave him a smug look. "If that's so, then why did I see her driving out of town just a few minutes ago?"

"She's taking a trip to New Orleans, since the weather's bad. A research trip. Maybe even a trip to the shooting range for practice. But don't worry, she'll be back by nightfall."

Sheriff Blanchard's expression grew angry at Brian's mention of the shooting range. Good, Brian thought. The implication hadn't been lost on the man. Brian could see the sheriff's jaw flexing and knew he was struggling with a response.

Sheriff Blanchard rose from the stool and laid some money on the counter. "Don't say I didn't warn you. That house is the root of all evil in this town, and the problems won't stop until you leave it alone. You barge in here and disrespect the beliefs of the people here and you pay the price. There's nothing I can do about that."

Sheriff Blanchard walked out of the café and into the rain, letting the door slam shut behind him. Brian turned back to the counter where Tom had placed his breakfast. "I'm making all kinds of people happy this morning," Brian said.

Tom stared out the plate-glass window of the café, his expression serious. "He's right about one thing, you know."

"Oh, yeah? What's that?"

"About you offending the people here by disrespecting their beliefs."

"Maybe if I understood exactly what beliefs I'm disrespecting, I could stop."

Tom shook his head. "Most every generation of people in this town for over one hundred years has believed the Borque estate was cursed. People believe no woman can occupy the house again without bringing the evil spirits back. I know the research woman is just here doing her job, same as the writer woman was, but them being here alone is enough to rile up the townsfolk."

"What are they afraid of?"

Tom looked directly at Brian, a tiny hint of fear in his eyes. "According to legend, they're afraid that those women will unknowingly unlock the gates of hell and that all of Cypriere will be swallowed up in its wake."

Chapter Fourteen

Justine dug into her purse with one hand, trying to find her ringing cell phone without taking her eyes off the road. The rain had lessened since she'd gotten on the highway, but it was still the sort of conditions that required attention. Finally, her hand found the cold metal piece and she pulled it out to check the display.

Her mother.

The one person in the world she least felt like talking to at the moment, and also the person she was on her way to see. The ironies of life. She didn't want to deal with her but she needed her, as she had a million other times in her life. Maybe this time her mother would actually come through.

Brian had seemed mildly surprised when Justine had told him she was seeking information from a voodoo priestess. She couldn't help but wonder how much more surprised he'd be to find out that woman was her mother and she was locked away in an assisted-living center.

She tossed the phone on the passenger seat. She'd know what her mother wanted soon enough. The exit for downtown New Orleans was just ahead, so she turned on her blinker and eased her car over to the exit. A million thoughts rolled through her head and none of them good. Dealing with her mother was never a straightforward process. It was always a guessing game to try and figure out how to coax information out of Ava, and then you had to decipher her ramblings into some sort of sense, if there was any.

Justine pulled into the parking lot of the assisted-living center and parked in a space near the front entry. She took in a huge breath and let it out slowly before exiting the car and entering the center.

The young receptionist smiled at her as she entered the lobby. "It's been a while since I've seen you," the young woman said.

"I'm working on a project out of town. I'm only back for the day. Has she been any trouble?"

The receptionist waved a hand in dismissal. "Just being her usual self. I know it bothers you, but all of us here are used to it." The girl stopped talking and frowned. "Although Hilda said she was pitching a fit something fierce yesterday."

"About what?"

"About you. Probably a good thing you got a day off. Maybe seeing you will calm her back down." She gave Justine an encouraging smile and pressed the buzzer to unlock the secured area.

"Thanks," Justine said, and stepped into the hallway. The door shut behind her and the sound of the lock clicking into place echoed in the stark white hall. She walked halfway down the hall and stopped in front of a closed door. Room number Twelve. Originally, Ava had been assigned room Thirteen, but she'd had such a breakdown when she saw the number printed on the door that the staff moved room Twelve's original resident into Thirteen to make room for her mother.

Steeling her emotions against the assault that she knew was coming, she opened the door and stepped inside her mother's room. Ava sat in a rocking chair next to the window, staring outside at the rain. Her silver-and-black hair was long and wiry, giving her the appearance of the witches one read about in fiction. Justine had always thought that was intentional on her part. Her mother liked to have power over other people, even if through fear.

Even though she was only fifty-six years old, Ava looked old enough to be Justine's grandmother. Years of medical issues and drug abuse had aged her body. The gray hair had been there as long as Justine could remember, but Ava had never colored it.

"Mother," Justine said.

She didn't respond at first, and Justine wondered if she was asleep. It was odd to see, but her mother had the ability to sleep completely upright. It had unnerved more than one person in her lifetime. She stepped closer to the rocking chair and her mother slowly turned her head away from the window.

"I see you finally remembered you had a mother," Ava said, her voice low and raspy.

"I told you I would be working out of town," Justine reminded her. "My cell phone doesn't get good reception there, especially on days like today."

Her mother looked at her with black eyes that seemed to see straight through her. "The spirits prefer the darkness of the storm. They thicken the air."

Justine didn't bother pointing out that the storm was responsible for clogging up the airwaves. Her mother wouldn't hear it, and Justine had given up futile arguments long ago. She sat on the end of Ava's bed. "I need to ask you some questions about the Borque family. Do you remember telling me about them?"

Her mother was silent for a couple of seconds and Justine was afraid she'd lapsed into one of her bouts of lost memory, but finally she nodded. "I remember. They were a cursed family. Betrayal and greed brought on their deaths…released the curse."

"Franklin Borque brought on their deaths."

"He was obsessed with the lion, but Marilyn stole it from him. Stole what mattered most, and he brought the spirits down on her."

"Do you know what Marilyn did with the emeralds?"

Ava frowned. "I don't know of any emeralds."

"The emeralds from the lion statue. The voodoo woman contained them and Marilyn hid them where they couldn't do evil any longer."

Ava stared blankly at her. "The lion…it was the lion."

Justine bit her lower lip, trying to control her frustration. They'd reached the same impasse the last time she'd asked her mother about the stones. For whatever reason, her memories now seemed to stop with the lion.

Ava turned her head to look back out the window. "'Water, water everywhere…'"

Justine sighed. "The Rime of the Ancient Mariner" had always been her mother's favorite. "Mother. The Borques, remember? What did Marilyn do with the emeralds?"

Ava continued to stare outside. "I don't know any Borques, honey. You must be mistaken."

Justine saw her mother's eyes close and knew she'd gotten everything out of her that she could for now. Maybe for good. Ava hadn't told Justine the story of the cursed lion since she was a little girl, no matter how many times she'd tried to get more information. Justine had never been able to make a connection until Olivia had contacted her for the job at laMalediction. Her mother had claimed the story was an old family tale, but until now, Justine had been unable to produce a lead.

Justine's first thought when speaking to Olivia was

that perhaps her mother's family had been servants in the Borque household, but when Olivia told Justine about the diaries and Marilyn Borque's illegitimate child, Justine had the overwhelming feeling that her mother hadn't descended from servants but from Marilyn Borque herself.

She rose from the bed and leaned over to kiss her mother on the cheek. Ava didn't even stir. Justine left the room and continued farther down the hall to the nurse's station. Hilda looked up at her from the desk and smiled, her bright white teeth shining against her dark, aged skin.

"I'm glad to see you, child."

"I heard Mother was acting up."

Hilda nodded. "She sorely tested my patience yesterday. Wasn't nothing going to calm her down but my calling you. I tried to tell her that it went straight to voice mail, but she was in a bad way. Insisting you was surrounded by evil and had to be rescued. Raised all kinds of hell, wanting me to call the police."

Justine stared. "Ava wanted you to call the police?" Hilda knew her mother's history with the police.

"Surprised the hell out of me, too, but the only way I could get her to take her meds was by promising to call them. Doctor Murphy gave her something to help her sleep, and by this morning, I'm sure she's forgotten all about the police part, which is just as well, since I wasn't about to call them and report a haunting, or whatever she called it."

"Why didn't you leave me a message yesterday? I would have gotten it eventually."

"Oh, honey, if I would have thought there was something to it, I would have. But I knew you were out of town working. There was no sense bothering you over one of your mother's spells. There's going to be a lot more of them before she leaves this world."

"But you called this morning."

Hilda nodded. "She forgot about calling the police, not about calling you. Started nagging me first thing this morning. I made her wait until a decent hour and told her I'd leave a message when I didn't get you, but she said not to. Said you were already on your way here."

Justine stared at Hilda. "I haven't talked to her in days, and I didn't decide to come until this morning. How could she possibly know that?"

"I've spent thirty years working with people here. People that was not long for this world. Seen some mighty strange things in my time. Things I can't explain by this world's standards."

"You think she sees things?"

"I think maybe, when you're close to the other side, you see things that fully alive people can't."

"How much longer?"

Hilda sighed. "The doctor says the valves in her heart's all but gone. Maybe a month. Maybe two."

The breath caught in Justine's throat. "Thanks," she managed to say, and walked out of the clinic with a backward wave at the receptionist.

She slid into the driver's seat of her car and clutched the steering wheel, staring out the windshield at the dark, rainy sky that exactly matched her feelings. Justine had issues with her mother, that was certain, and no one would ever accuse her of not having the right to…no one who knew their history, anyway. But that didn't mean Justine couldn't understand the reasons behind the things her mother had done, even if she struggled every day with forgiving them.

Regardless of the past, Justine didn't want her mother to die, especially this way. Locked away in a facility with white walls and locks on the door. The exact same way she'd spent much of her life. There had been bouts of good times, when it seemed as if the doctors had found the right combination of meds and therapy to make her normal, but they'd never been able to keep her that way. No matter the type of medication, Ava's strange internal system eventually built up an immunity to it and she slipped slowly back into madness. Now the lucid moments were so rare that Justine didn't hold any hope of getting useful information from her any longer, but at least she'd tried.

Justine started the car and left the facility for the library. The library had free internet and a ton of source books she could utilize for her research into the Borque family tree. With any luck, she might already have the email from John, which should give her a good starting point.

BRIAN DROVE DOWN the narrow street to the rental house, mulling over the exchanges he'd had in the café. He hoped Justine had better luck with her research than he had so far. All he'd seemed to manage was to scare people or piss them off. Neither was a big help, although Chris Pauley was now at the top of his list of people he wanted to take a closer look at.

He saw the curtains on the house next to the rental fall back in place as he pulled into the driveway. What had the sheriff said the woman's name was, the one who heard the alarm? Bergeron maybe? Yeah, that was it.

He stepped out of the Jeep and hurried across the front lawn to the house next door, not surprised in the least when a tiny old woman answered the door almost immediately.

"Mrs. Bergeron?"

The woman gave him a suspicious look. "It's 'Miss.' Never had the displeasure of putting up with a man."

This was going well. "My name is Brian Marcentel. I'm renting the house next door."

"I know who you are. Living in sin with that woman that ain't your wife."

Brian was momentarily taken aback. That was something he hadn't yet been accused of this morning. "We're not living in sin, ma'am. We're both working for the Borque estate. We sleep in separate bedrooms."

She didn't look the least bit convinced.

"I swear," he said and raised one hand, wondering if she would get a Bible for the other.

"Hmmmpf." She frowned, but stepped back and motioned him inside. "If you got something to say, best say it inside. That cool air bothers my arthritis."

Brian stepped inside and pulled the door shut behind him. Miss Bergeron was in a small kitchen just to the right of the front door, and motioned for him to take a seat at a tiny dining table.

"I was just fixing some tea. Tea's good in chilly weather and doesn't stain my false teeth as bad as coffee." She poured a cup of tea into a dainty porcelain cup and placed it in front of Brian, then poured one for herself and took a seat across from him.

Brian dumped an unprecedented amount of sugar in the cup, hoping to drown out the taste of the tea, which he hated. He knew better than to try and get out of drinking it altogether, especially if he was hoping to get information out of the woman.

"I don't cotton much to gossip," Miss Bergeron said, "or living outside the good Lord's word, but I've seen the lights on in both bedrooms at night, so I figure you're speaking the truth. Still, it doesn't look right, two young people staying together in such close quarters."

"No, ma'am. I can see where people would get the wrong idea. I'm glad you gave me a chance to explain."

"Well, you seem like a decent enough young man. How's the tea?"

Brian took a sip and tried not to grimace. "Lovely, thanks. Miss Bergeron, at the café this morning, Sheriff Blanchard said you told him you heard the trouble last night. Did you hear the window break?"

"Yes. My first thought was that stray dog had tipped over the trash again, but then I heard that alarm and I knew it wasn't dogs that had set it off."

"Did you look outside?"

"Of course. Daddy taught all us girls how to shoot a shotgun, and I'm not afraid to use one. One of my bedroom windows faces that house, but I couldn't see anything in the storm." She frowned and looked down at her tea.

Brian immediately picked up on her uncertainty. "Are you sure you didn't see anything? Even if you're not certain what it was?"

She stirred her tea for a couple seconds more, then sighed. "Well, I don't guess it can possibly hurt, but I thought I saw something white moving in the woods just behind the house."

"An animal?"

"No. It was far too tall to be an animal, but what person in their right mind would be running around in a storm like that?"

"Kids maybe," Brian said, throwing out the sheriff's favorite catchall.

"You've been listening to Sheriff Blanchard too long. He used to be a good lawman, but the closer he gets to retirement, the lazier he gets. Blames everything on kids because he doesn't want to get up off his rear and do some work."

Brian began to warm to his somewhat crotchety neighbor. "So you don't think it was kids."

"If you were asking me do I think kids might chuck something through your window for fun, then I'd say sure they would. But even the kids in Cypriere's smart enough to come in out of a storm like what we had last night. And although I doubt we have any budding rocket scientists around here, I'd say they're all smart enough to wear dark colors if they're going around like a bunch of hooligans."

Brian nodded, unable to find a flaw in Miss Bergeron's logic. Funny how the little old lady seemed to have a better grip on the people of Cypriere than the man who was charged with protecting it.

Brian felt his cell phone vibrate in his pocket and pulled it out. It was a text from John asking him to call as soon as he could. He rose from the table. "You'll have to excuse me. This is a work call that I need to take. I appreciate you taking the time to talk to me, Miss Bergeron. If you need anything, please don't hesitate to ask."

Miss Bergeron snorted. "I ain't the one with all the trouble, but I appreciate the offer. Shows your mamma raised you with some manners and respect for your elders." She followed Brian to the door and closed it behind him.

Brian pressed in John's number as he ran across the lawn and let himself into the rental house.

"Are you drowning out there yet?" John asked as soon as Brian answered the phone.

"Almost. This place certainly has its share of spectacular storms."

"I guess you're stuck at the rental, right? Is there somewhere you can talk where you can't be heard?"

Brian perked up. "Justine left this morning for New

Orleans to do some research on the voodoo angle. Did you find something?"

"No. And that's the problem. Before ten years ago, Justine Chatry didn't exist. No driver's license, school records, birth records…it's like she appeared out of nowhere at age eighteen."

Brian sank onto the living room couch, trying to absorb what John had said. "But she went to college in New Orleans. They must have school records if she was admitted."

"She claimed she was homeschooled and tested out of all her basic classes for entry. I don't like it, Brian. Don't get me wrong, since she materialized out of thin air, Justine's clean as a whistle. Not even a traffic ticket."

"Which is almost suspicious in itself."

"Almost," John agreed.

"Did you find any family? Anyone listed as next of kin on paperwork?"

"Not a soul. I even got a buddy of mine to pull her phone records. She calls work, Chinese takeout and some assisted-living center, but there's no one there with her last name. I figure maybe that's work-related, too, as she mostly does ancestry research and work with antiques."

Brian rose from the couch and paced across the living room and kitchen area. John had been very thorough, but something didn't feel right. Something he couldn't quite put his finger on.

"You still there, buddy?" John asked.

"Yeah," Brian said, and opened the pantry door to grab a protein bar. "Just trying to make sense of it."

He pulled a protein bar out of the box and stuck the box back in the pantry, next to the jars of spaghetti sauce. And that's when it hit him. Why Justine had looked so familiar when they were eating spaghetti.

"Did she only call one assisted-living center?"

"I think so. Hold on…yeah, only that one. You think something's there?"

"Maybe. Give me that number."

John read off the number and Brian wrote it down on a pad of paper on the kitchen counter.

"What are you thinking?" John asked.

"I'd rather not say until I know for sure. It's just a hunch, and a real thin one. I'll call you back if I get anything."

"Sounds good," John said, and rang off.

Brian tore the phone number off the notepad and paced the length of the front rooms twice before stopping. He stared at the number, wanting to call, but afraid of what he'd find. It couldn't be, right? The odds of running into her after all these years were a million-to-one.

Before he could change his mind, he pressed in the number for the assisted-living facility. "May I speak to Ava Comeaux?" he asked when the receptionist answered.

"I'm sorry, sir," the receptionist replied, "but she had a rough night and the doctor gave her a sedative. She'll probably be out for several hours. Would you like me to tell her you called?"

"No, thank you," Brian managed before he ended the call.

He slumped onto the couch and placed his phone and the paper on the coffee table. What in God's name was he supposed to do now? No wonder Justine had been so skittish and secretive. No wonder she'd avoided him as much as possible. She must have recognized him from the beginning and lived in constant fear that he'd recognize her. That's why she seemed so afraid that night at dinner, when he commented that she seemed familiar.

It was twenty years ago, but he could still remember that night as if it was yesterday. He was just sitting down to spaghetti dinner with his mom and dad when his uncle, the sheriff in their tiny bayou town, had called. There had been a house fire, and he rescued a little girl. He needed a safe place for her to stay until he could sort out the mess.

A deputy dropped the girl off at the house. She was eight years old and scared to death. The deputy explained that she'd escaped harm by hiding in the bedroom closet, and they discovered her before the fire moved to the back of the house. Her mother, the only other occupant, had been transported by helicopter to the hospital in New Orleans. The girl claimed they had no living relatives.

His mom had helped her wash her face and hands and finally convinced her to eat. She didn't talk and avoided looking directly at anyone, but Brian could tell she was hungry by the way she looked at the plate of food. He remembered wondering when the last time she'd eaten had been. Even though he was only ten himself, he'd helped his mom deliver food to the poor in their community every Saturday. He knew what hungry looked like.

The girl had tackled the spaghetti with a gusto that surprised all of them. His mother had quietly refilled her plate and the girl looked up at her with a shy smile, the same smile he'd seen that night he and Justine had eaten spaghetti for dinner. It couldn't possibly be a coincidence that the only number, aside from random fast food that Justine called on a regular basis, just happened to the facility that cared for Ava Comeaux. Ava had to be Justine's mother.

The woman who'd locked Justine in the bedroom closet and set fire to the house.

Chapter Fifteen

Justine powered up her laptop on a table in the back corner of the library. It was empty and quietly tucked away behind the rows of books, and Justine felt a semblance of security for the first time in days, which surprised her. She hadn't realized until entering the library just how uneasy Cypriere made her feel. She'd tried to maintain a professional perspective about the job and the location and thought she'd succeeded, but apparently, she'd only been fooling herself. Clearly the job unnerved her more than she'd wanted to admit.

She logged on to the internet and saw that John's email was the first in her inbox. She took a deep breath in and slowly blew it out before clicking on the email and opening the attached file. The documents had scanned clearly and were easy to read. Wheeler's organization had fortunately not been affected by his mental state and Justine easily scanned through the documents, tying them all together.

He'd definitely done his research. The surveys he'd paid for indicated huge amounts of oil on the estate property, and the offers he had on hold with oil companies were staggering. Even at collector's value, the price the cursed emeralds would fetch was negligible compared to the tens of millions that Wheeler was hoping to cash in on.

The last pages of the scan contained Wheeler's family-lineage research—birth and death certificates, with the final page containing a carefully constructed family tree. It had a couple of black squares, most likely where a spouse, sibling or child might exist, but he hadn't found the records to prove it yet. She started at the top of the page with Franklin Borque, and read every name indicated below him.

Philomene Bajoliere.

Justine's breath caught in her throat. Her hands shook as she located her own family research file on her laptop and opened it. She scanned the small list of names that she'd managed to tie to her mother. *Philomene Bajoliere.* The name was so uncommon, there was no chance it was a coincidence. She switched back to Wheeler's research to see exactly how that person was related to Wheeler.

A solid line connected Wheeler's father to his mother but a dotted line to the side of Wheeler's father connected with Philomene. Below Philomene's name was a box with the single word *bastard* written inside. Justine felt a wave of nausea pass over her, certain that her mother's name belonged in that box. The date below the box was the year her mother was born. Wheeler and her mother shared the same father.

Apparently, fathering illegitimate children ran in the family along with psychosis.

She leaned back in the library chair and stared at the shelves in front of her. Franklin Borque was her mother's great-great grandfather. She finally had the answers she'd been searching for all these years, and now it was the last thing she wanted.

A tear formed at the corner of her eye and spilled over onto her cheek. She swiped at it with one hand and reached out with the other to close the laptop. Her work in New

Orleans was done. She had every mile of the long drive back to Cypriere to figure out how to act normal.

Even though her life had never been normal and never would be.

BRIAN RAN ONE HAND ACROSS his short hair and blew out a breath, his heart aching for the scared little girl he'd met so briefly and the woman who had grown up with that night hanging over her. What in the world was he supposed to do now? There was no way he could pretend around her. He had to tell her he knew who she was, but he didn't want to tell her he'd had John poke into her background even more than they had already.

Justine had very logical and persuasive reasons for changing her name and erasing her past, and he didn't blame her one bit for her decision. Her mother's actions that night and her subsequent commitment to the mental hospital had made the New Orleans news and was well-known in towns even hundreds of miles away. People in Louisiana had long memories. The only way for Justine to escape the stigma of her childhood was to become someone else.

And now her carefully constructed identity had been undermined by a spaghetti dinner.

He rose from the couch and grabbed his keys. The nearest hardware store was forty miles away, but he needed to get out of the house for a while. Buying a new window for the bedroom was as good an excuse as any. Sometime during his window-repair adventure, he needed to come up with a way to tell Justine what he knew.

As he walked out the door, a thought jolted through his mind and he drew up short. The notes. The smell of smoke on the first night at laMalediction. No wonder Justine was so rattled.

Someone in Cypriere knew exactly who she was, too.

DARK CLOUDS LOOMED overhead as the sun began to sink behind the line of cypress trees. The rain started to fall as Justine approached the exit to Cypriere. She merged onto the exit and frowned at the swirling sky above. It was almost as if a permanent cloud of doom hung over the entire town. She glanced into her rearview mirror and her pulse quickened as a white car, about a half mile behind her, also took the exit.

The car had been on the same stretch of highway with her at least since she'd left New Orleans. There had also been a white car parked across the street from the assisted-living center, but Justine hadn't registered the exact make and model at the time, and hadn't even remembered it until she'd noticed the white car on the highway. For the first hour, it didn't seem so odd. Plenty of people traveled this stretch of highway, especially in the middle of the day; but as vehicles began to exit to connecting highways and town, she realized the white car was still with her.

She'd adjusted her speed to see if the car would pass or fall behind, but the driver had maintained the same distance regardless of her own speed. In the last ten miles of highway, all other traffic had exited the highway, leaving only Justine and the white car on the lonely stretch of road. She'd hoped when she exited for Cypriere that the white car continued past and she could chide herself for being paranoid, but that option no longer existed. And while it wasn't completely impossible that someone might also be driving from New Orleans to Cypriere at the same time of day as she, there was no good reason for the driver to match her speed.

She grabbed her cell phone and was relieved to see she had a signal. Now if only Brian was somewhere that he could hear his phone. The stretch of road between the highway and Cypriere was a narrow, lonely piece of blacktop that ran straight through the marsh, and there wasn't a single structure before reaching the town.

"Marcentel," Brian answered.

"It's Justine. Someone's following me."

"Where are you?" Brian's response was sharp and immediate.

"I just exited the highway for Cypriere. I think they've followed me all the way from New Orleans. There's a truck coming from Cypriere that's stopped at the underpass, but as soon as they get on the highway, I'll be alone."

Justine heard rustling on the phone for a second then a door slam.

"I'm headed your way now," Brian said. "Just keep driving normally. If the car begins to gain on you, speed up as fast as you can safely drive. We should intersect in twenty minutes."

"Okay," Justine said and turned right at the underpass and pressed the accelerator firmly down. She watched in her rearview mirror as the white car approached the underpass then turned right behind her. It was still a ways behind, but not the half-mile distance that it had been on the highway. She pressed the accelerator down a bit more and concentrated on navigating the winding road and alternating checking her rearview for the car.

Every time she checked, the car was closer than it had been before.

She glanced at the clock on her dashboard and felt her pulse increase. Only five minutes had passed since her phone call to Brian. She had another fifteen minutes to go until he reached her, and that was assuming the other driver didn't get to her before then. But another peek in her rearview didn't leave her much hope. The white car had closed half the distance between them and was gaining fast.

She hit Redial and pressed the speaker button, so she could keep both hands on the wheel to control the car as she barreled down the worn asphalt road.

"Are you okay?" The anxiety in Brian's voice was clear.

"No. The car is closing in on me. I'm going to leave the phone on speaker. Don't disconnect. If something happens, if I can see anything…I'll yell it to you."

"Don't think that way. I'm only ten minutes away."

Justine looked in her rearview and felt the blood drain from her face. The white car was only twenty yards behind her. "It's right behind me—he's going to hit me!"

Justine braced herself for the hit, but instead the car swung out to the side and pulled alongside her. She tried to make out the driver, but the window tint was too dark to see through. A second later, the car slammed into the driver's side of her vehicle.

Justine gripped the steering wheel so hard her hands ached, desperately trying to maintain control of the vehicle, but the front wheel dipped off the asphalt into the edge of a drainage ditch. The change in elevation was all it took to pitch the car off into the ditch.

As the car slammed to a stop, Justine screamed and threw her arms up in front of her face to protect it from the air bag that deployed. Water from the ditch splashed up, creating a solid sheet of water that fell over the car. She could hear Brian's voice on the cell phone, but it had slid to the floor at impact and she couldn't reach it.

Panicked, she moved the air bag to the side to look out the side window, and her heart sank. The white car had stopped just up the road from her and was now slowly backing toward her. She reached into her laptop bag for her pistol then tried to open her car door, but it was jammed shut. Gripping the pistol in her right hand, she lowered her driver's window and took aim at the white car.

Her first shot hit the rear window and shattered the glass. The car changed direction and sped away, tires squealing on the asphalt. Justine watched the car until it disappeared over a rise in the road about a half mile away, and then let her breath out in a whoosh, unaware that she'd been holding it.

She looked down at her watch and took a deep breath, trying to calm her racing heart. Five more minutes and Brian would be there. She hoped it was soon enough.

"DAMN IT!" The sound of the gunshot rang out through Brian's cell phone and he pressed the accelerator down even farther, gripping the steering wheel to control the Jeep as it slid around a corner on the worn road. When he got on a straight stretch of road, he picked up his phone again to see if Justine would reply, but he got only silence.

What the hell had happened?

If something happened to Justine, it was his fault. He should have made her leave. Should have told John that the research would have to be done in New Orleans, with only occasional visits to the estate until he could figure out exactly what he and Justine had stepped into the middle of.

Now she might be injured…or worse.

He shook his head and concentrated on driving. Thinking that way was something he couldn't allow himself. He had to focus on the mission. Extract the soldier and get her to safety. Identify and destroy the enemy—*now.* This was war.

He turned onto the stretch of road where he expected to find Justine and sucked in a breath when he didn't see her car anywhere. The evening sun had almost set, and the light had all but faded from the road, leaving only dim light and his headlights to illuminate the road in front of him. He scanned the sides of the road as he drove, and almost passed her car before he saw it in the drainage ditch. His heart leaped into his throat as he screeched to a halt, then ran from the Jeep to the ditch, calling her name.

The car was empty, but the driver's window was down. "Justine!" He scanned the woods, starting to panic, when he heard a voice behind him.

"I'm here," Justine said, and exited the woods from the other side of the road. "I figured if the car came back they'd look for me on that side of the road, so I hid on the other."

She waded through the ditch, clutching her laptop bag, and he ran across the road to give her a hand crawling out of the channel. "Are you all right? I heard a gunshot. What happened?" He scanned her for any sign of injury and felt a wave of relief pass over him when all he saw was mud and water.

"I'm okay. Just a little shaken up."

"I'm sure. Let's get the hell out of here. You can tell me what happened on the way."

"My car—"

"I'll call a tow company in New Orleans to come get it. Do you need anything out of it?"

"No. I grabbed my laptop and my pistol when I crawled out. My cell phone got wet when water started to seep into the car. It's shot."

They climbed into the Jeep and Brian took off, constantly checking his mirrors and the road ahead for an ambush. Justine relayed her story as he drove, and his anxiety level increased with every turn of phrase. No way was this random. And in order to make it happen, someone must have followed Justine to New Orleans and then back to Cypriere, just waiting for the right opportunity to strike.

But all the people he suspected were in the café this morning after Justine left.

The revelation from John's information flashed through his mind. Someone in Cypriere knew who Justine really was, and her mother wouldn't be that hard to find. The stalker could have waited at the assisted-care facility, figuring that Justine would visit her mother while she was in New Orleans. They wouldn't necessarily have had to follow her from Cypriere.

But to force her car off the road was bold, which meant he was more desperate. The worst thing was, Brian still had no idea why Justine was such a threat.

"I think you need to reconsider leaving," Brian said when she finished recounting her tale. "He's going to continue escalating until he gets what he wants, and all I can figure is that right now, he wants us to leave."

Justine shook her head. "I'm not leaving until the job is done. If anything, this just made me angry. I mean, it frightened me. But then, that makes me angry, since that's exactly what he intended to do."

Brian struggled with his feelings, wavering between admiration at her strength and dismay at her hardheadedness. "I'll have to tell Olivia and John."

"Do you think they'll make me leave?"

"I think they'll trust me to handle the situation in the manner I think is best. Right now, if you want to stay, then I'm willing to try and make it work, but we're going to have to change our strategy."

Justine gave Brian an apprehensive look. "Should we call our friend, Sheriff Blanchard?"

"No. I'll call John and get the state police involved in a covert way. I'd rather keep this suppressed as much as possible, to throw the stalker off balance. But if you're not okay with that, I understand, and we'll figure out another way."

"So you want to pretend nothing happened…to piss him off?"

"Yeah. I think it will force him to act sooner than planned, and perhaps in acting without a plan, he'll make a mistake."

"That makes sense."

"We'll be extra cautious. I know you don't like me looking over your shoulder, but I'm going to have to maintain a closer presence than I have. No more road trips alone. We go everywhere together from this point forward."

"You'll get no argument out of me."

Her words, and the fact that she was so quick to respond, let Brian know that today's attack had shaken Justine more than she would ever admit. The truth was, it had shaken him, too, but it had angered him even more.

Chapter Sixteen

Lightning flashed in the dark sky as they pulled into the driveway, but the rain Justine expected hadn't begun to fall. Brian scanned the area as he parked, and glanced up at the sky.

"It's holding off for now," he said.

"The calm before the storm," Justine said as she collected her laptop and climbed out of the Jeep. She entered the rental house and dumped her laptop on the dining table she was using for her work, then headed into her bedroom to grab a change of clothes. She was starting to chill from wading through the ditch and wanted to take a hot shower while Brian conducted his exterior patrol of the rental house and grounds.

Eyeing herself critically in the bathroom mirror, she decided she didn't look nearly as bad as she felt. Her skin was a little pale, but she hadn't sustained any injuries from the wreck, not any visible ones anyway. The attack, on top of her visit with her mother, along with what she'd learned about her lineage, was a lot for one person to handle at a time, but she didn't have a choice.

If she broke down, Brian would probably discover her secret and make her leave. She'd never finish her research—never know with certainty that her mom's stories and Wheeler's research were accurate and that she was a descendant of Franklin Borque.

If she could just find the emeralds, the estate settlement would prompt DNA testing for all potential heirs. Assuming Franklin Borque was buried on the estate, Justine could petition for a definitive answer. Without a claim on the estate, the attorney would never approve an exhumation and DNA test for her.

So all she needed to do right now was keep from looking generally miserable and scared or bursting into tears. If she could manage that, she might be able to pull off the evening. With any luck, the storm would break tonight and they'd be back at laMalediction tomorrow. It was easier to focus with more square footage between her and Brian.

Ten minutes later she stepped out of the shower, pleased to see that the steamy water had returned some of the color to her face. She heard the front door of the rental house open and close, and took a deep breath before leaving the bathroom. It was now or never. Brian would want to know if she'd learned anything on her field trip. Putting off giving him the information would seem strange, especially in light of the attack. He would assume her research may be relevant.

Brian was washing his hands in the kitchen sink and looked up at her when she walked into the living room. "I got the bedroom window replaced this afternoon, but still need to do some caulking. It's still covered with the tarp for now. With any luck, the rain will break soon and I can finish up."

"I heard the weather report on the way in from New Orleans. They seem to think we'll get a break, but you know how reliable that can be." She grabbed a bottled water from the refrigerator, then took a seat on the couch.

Brian dried his hands on a dishtowel. "Did John send you the information from Wheeler's office?"

"Yeah," Justine replied, trying to keep her voice calm. "I'll print off the file so we can take a look and see if any names jump out at us. Did you find out anything at the café this morning that can help?"

"Ha. This is one strange town. It almost seems like people are either too scared or too offended to talk. It's a real trial trying to get something useful out of them." He walked into the living room and sat in the chair across from her. "I want to check into that mechanic a little more. He's got a chip on his shoulder that I can't put my finger on, and our friend Sheriff Blanchard was his usual cheerful self."

"What about Tom?"

"Same as always. Expects death and despair from the spirits." Brian sighed. "I did find out that he used to own one of those cabins along the bayou that back up to the trail to laMalediction. In fact, he just sold it to our friendly mechanic. I was trying to casually get the other cabin owners' names from him when the sheriff interrupted. Then I couldn't find a good way to work back into the conversation."

"Maybe you can try again tomorrow."

"Maybe. What about you? Any luck with the voodoo woman?"

Justine shook her head, trying to temper the disappointment and sadness that began to overwhelm her every time she thought of her mother. "Not really. She's…she's not well, really. She remembered the story of the lion statue, but I couldn't get more out of her."

"Alzheimer's?"

She dropped her gaze to the floor. "Something like that."

"How long does your mother have?"

Tears immediately formed in her eyes and she sucked in a breath. "How did you find out?"

"I remembered."

She looked up at him and the compassion in his eyes was all it took to send her tears spilling over. "It was the spaghetti, wasn't it?"

"That's why I remembered, yeah. That night when you smiled, sitting there with spaghetti sauce on the collar of your shirt, something flashed in my mind. I just couldn't place it, but earlier today it clicked into place."

Justine swiped at the tears on her cheeks with her hand. "I didn't want you to remember. I didn't want anyone to know."

"But someone already does—here in Cypriere."

Justine nodded. "That's what it looks like." She told him about the picture of her mother in a straitjacket that had been left in her room the first night in the house.

"There's no way they recognized you that quickly, found that picture and snuck into laMalediction in the same day. You realize that means someone has been keeping track of you for a long time—knew you were coming to laMalediction before you ever got here."

"I know. I just don't understand why. I just want to forget the past and move on. Why keep dredging it up? Why keep track of me, just waiting for an opportunity to bring up my horrible past?"

Brian moved over to the couch to sit beside her, and placed his hand on hers. "I understand."

Justine shook her head. "You couldn't possibly."

"You're right. I can't understand the level and depth of your pain, but I do understand being so embarrassed by what others have done that you want to become someone else."

"You had the perfect family. I could tell that night, just from that short amount of time I spent there. Your parents were great."

Brian nodded. "But my uncle wasn't. Right before his scheduled retirement, he was investigated by the state. They found that he'd repeatedly abused inmates, beating them and sometimes raping the women. He'd been on the take with every illegal business in town."

Justine sat upright. "You're kidding. Someone finally believed a complaint about your saintly uncle?"

Brian's expression shifted from sympathetic to horrified. "Oh, no, don't tell me...your mother... Oh, hell. How bad?"

"You don't want to know. He convinced the hospital that she'd done it to herself. Given the entirety of her actions that night, they believed him."

"Justine, I am so sorry. I don't even know what to say."

He was so clearly miserable, Justine felt her heart go out to him. It was hard not to feel guilty for the actions of those close to you. She knew that in spades. "It's not your fault. You were just a child. Nothing that happened to our family or that our family members did was our fault."

"But the stigma follows you. I don't blame you for changing your identity. I would have done the same thing." He took a deep breath and blew it out. "We had to move after news of my uncle's exploits made it through town, which was about ten minutes after his arrest, given the size of the place. Our house was vandalized and we received hate mail. My dad got a job transfer to another town and we moved. Fortunately, he was my mom's brother, so we didn't share a last name. I can't imagine what the New Orleans Police Department would think if they ever made the connection."

He looked Justine straight in the eyes. "And none of that compares at all with what *you* must have gone through. Still go through, dealing with her. I don't know how I'd feel if I were you."

"I don't know how to feel most of the time. I love her but I hate what she is, even though I know it's the disease that made her do the things she did. I sometimes resent the burden of seeing to her care, because she wasn't there to see to mine, but I feel horrible that she's dying and her life was so bad." The emotional dam in Justine burst open and a few sobs slipped through.

Brian gathered her in his arms, holding her close to him as she cried. "Of course you feel bad," Brian whispered as he stroked her back. "You never had an opportunity for normal, and neither did she."

The heat from Brian's body warmed Justine, as did his words. She'd expected…anger, repulsion…she wasn't sure. What she had not anticipated was empathy, especially from the nephew of one of her mother's abusers. The fact that they'd both been hurt by the man made his words mean that much more.

She took a breath to regain control, and pushed back just a bit so that she could look at him. "I really appreciate your understanding. I'm sorry I didn't trust you with this earlier."

Brian reached one hand up to wipe a stray tear from her cheek. "You didn't know you could trust me, especially given the past. I hope you know now that you can."

Justine nodded.

Brian's eyes were locked on hers, his arms still held her close, and even before he lowered his lips to hers, she knew he was going to kiss her. And she knew she wasn't going to pull away. But the way her body responded, the heat that rose from her core, was something she hadn't expected. Never before had she experienced such a heady feeling from one man's touch.

She returned his kiss with a passion she didn't know she had, and when he parted her lips with his tongue, she felt her heart beat faster. He trailed kisses down her neck to the sensitive skin on her shoulders and she moaned.

"I want you, Justine," Brian whispered, his voice husky.

"Yes," Justine managed.

He lifted her effortlessly from the couch and carried her to his bedroom. He slowly relieved her of her clothes, kissing every square inch of her body before he lowered her onto the bed. White-hot heat burned from her core as she watched him undress, and her body tingled with anticipation as he rolled on a condom and moved over her.

He lowered his head to kiss her long and deep, and entered her with a single thrust.

Justine cried out as pleasure rushed through her body. She clutched his back and pulled him deeper into her, lifting her hips to match his stride. Her mind was almost hazy with the intensity of the joining, her body aching for the release she knew was coming. She could feel it building in her with every thrust, and she dug her nails into his back when she was perched just on the edge.

Brian paused for only a moment before he plunged one last time and sent them both over the brink.

BRIAN LAY BACK ON THE BED, his arm curled around Justine, who lay with her head in the crook of his shoulder. Their bodies fit together as if they were designed for each other, just as they had when making love. Brian had been aware of his attraction to Justine from the beginning, but even in his wildest dreams, he'd never imagined a joining like he and Justine had experienced. It was different from being with any other woman—the intensity, the passion was something he'd never felt before.

She was so different from any other woman he'd ever known—so many layers, and all of them shaping who she was today. Justine Chatry was the kind of woman a man could spend every day of his life discovering something about, and the fact that all of it wouldn't be pleasant only showed her strength of character and made her that much more attractive. There were so many things he wanted to ask her right now, but he was afraid of ruining the moment.

"You want to know about my mother," Justine said quietly, "but you won't ask because you don't want to upset me."

Brian stared down at her. "How… I didn't…"

"I'm not a mind reader, if that's what you're wondering. I don't share my mother's beliefs or her self-perceived skills. It's just that, if I were you, I'd want to know."

"How ill is she?"

"Terminal. The doctors give her a month, or maybe two. The valves in her heart are shot and her organs are failing. Perhaps from all the drugs she's been prescribed over the years. Perhaps from her own self-medicating. No matter. She's not eligible for transplants, and even if she was, her heart wouldn't stand the surgery required."

"I'm sorry."

"Me, too. It's a horrible way to die. I guess the only comfort I have is in knowing that her mental state protects her from knowing the worst of it. She's rarely coherent anymore."

"What about your father? Does he help with her at all?"

"I don't know who my father is. I'm not sure my mother does, either. My mother would take her medication for a while, and once she felt better she'd stop. Most men aren't interested in that big of a personality swing in their mate, especially not from day to day."

Brian shook his head, trying to grasp how hard it must have been for Justine, growing up in that household. The men her mother dated could escape, but Justine was only a child. "Who raised you, you know…after?"

"A nurse who'd cared for my mother in the institution. She told social services she was my aunt, but that wasn't the truth. No one knows much about my mother's past. She was a good woman, the nurse, and she and her husband did everything they could to see that I got a second chance at a normal life."

"They sound wonderful."

"They were."

"Were?"

"Yeah, they were killed in a car accident about five years ago. A hit-and-run. The cops never caught the guy who did it."

Brian let out a sigh. Yet another case of the police failing Justine completely. And Justine had been essentially left alone in the world, yet again. "That sucks. You've had to deal with so much, and yet you're so accomplished, so together. Most people would have fallen apart. You're a special woman, Justine."

Justine looked up at him and he could see tears glistening in the corner of her eyes. He stroked her face with one hand and leaned down to kiss her. As his lips touched hers, he felt whole, complete, and he gathered her into his arms as the kiss deepened.

Chapter Seventeen

Justine awakened the next morning to the sound of bacon frying. She opened her eyes and was momentarily startled when she didn't recognize the room. Then she remembered she was in a rental house in Cypriere. In Brian's bedroom. Brian's bed. The sheets around her smelled of his after-shave mixed with her shampoo, and memories of the night before flooded her mind.

She'd never felt so completely consumed with a man, and yet so comfortable with the thought of it. Brian was so strong and so gentle, so firm in his beliefs, yet so understanding of others. Add all his internal strengths to the very sexy external male, and it was one powerfully attractive package.

And one who deserves better than the dismal future you have to offer.

The thought ripped through her mind and she felt a wave of nausea pass over her. What had she done? She'd opened her heart and mind to a man, now knowing with certainty that any kind of future was impossible. No way would she drag another human being down with her, especially one she cared about. Brian deserved so much more than to be in the same position with his lover that she'd endured as a child with her mother.

Even worse, she was still lying to him and had spent the

night with him without telling him the truth. She climbed out of bed and found her clothes where Brian had laid them, across a chair in the corner of the room. Always so thoughtful. So caring. If only things could be different. Brian almost made her want to take the risk, but for his sake she couldn't. She pulled on her jeans and T-shirt and tried to get her thoughts under control. As far as she was concerned, last night was a huge mistake that should have never happened, and couldn't happen again.

Now all she had to do was convince him of something she didn't even believe herself.

She walked down the hall and paused just before entering the living room to focus. Then she stepped into the living room, determined to set everything back to the way it was before.

"Morning." Brian smiled as she crossed the room and slid onto a stool at the kitchen counter. He poured her a cup of coffee and placed it in front of her. "I know you usually get up earlier, but you were sleeping so well, I didn't have the heart to wake you."

Justine added artificial sweetener to the coffee and took a drink of the strong brew. "That's okay. If I didn't need the sleep, I would have awakened."

"I'm the same way. You want some breakfast? The bacon's done, and I was going to scramble some eggs to go with it."

"Sounds good," Justine said, trying to keep her voice from sounding strained. It was too homey—sitting there drinking coffee while Brian made breakfast for them. Too comfortable.

"I could get used to this," Brian said as he scrambled eggs in a skillet.

Justine froze. Everything about this was wrong, and she had to put a stop to it before Brian got any more ideas about the future that was not going to happen. "Brian, I…I think last night was great in some ways, but it was also a huge mistake." She stared down at her coffee.

He stopped stirring the eggs and several excruciating seconds of dead silence followed. "Is that really how you feel—that showing genuine emotion is a mistake? Somehow wrong? I won't deny that I'm attracted to you and care about you. What are you afraid of?"

Justine looked up at him. His eyes showed both the hurt and anger he felt, which made her feel even worse. But didn't absolve her from what she needed to do. "With everything you know about my mother, you have to ask what I'm afraid of? You're a smart guy, Brian. I'm sure you can figure it out."

Brian moved the skillet off the hot burner. "You're afraid of what people think of your mother? I already know who she is. How does that have any bearing on me and you?"

"I think it has bearing on who I could become. No one deserves to deal with that—especially with someone they love."

His eyes widened. "You think you'll become like her? Justine, I don't know what to say. Given your mother's undocumented past, you have no idea what contributed to her mental illness. To assume she was born with it is already a stretch, but to think you inherited the gene is absurd, especially with no proof."

"Really? So you'd be willing to take that risk? Willing to marry, buy a house, have kids with someone who could be a ticking time bomb?"

"I just don't see it that way. You have no medical reason to believe that you'll develop the same issues. You're restricting your entire life, based on a thread."

Justine bit her lip. His suggestion that she was acting

foolish bothered her even though he wasn't working with a full set of information. Given the earnest look on his face, he wasn't going to give up without it. She took a deep breath and blurted out, "I kept something else from you. Something I suspected before but wasn't able to verify until yesterday."

Brian's expression shifted to one of unease. "What?"

"I think I'm a descendant of the Borques. When the news stories about laMalediction broke, my mom got agitated and started talking in snippets of the past. When Olivia contacted me for the job, some of the details she provided sounded the same as some of my mother's lifelong ramblings."

"So you took the job but never told Olivia why." A flush started at the base of Brian's neck and moved slowly up his face. "You used us—all of us, for your own agenda."

Justine struggled to control her own anger at his words. After all, he wasn't entirely wrong. "Olivia also asked me to research the family tree as part of my job, so my 'agenda' aligned with what I was hired to do. Since when is wanting to know one's family lineage a horrible thing?"

Brian started to reply and she held up one hand to stop him. "And before you make a comment about inheritance, remember that I didn't know anything about the estate until you gave me the details. This is not about money. I don't want anything to do with this tainted mess."

Brian frowned. "Then why?"

Justine sighed. "I hoped that if I could trace my mother's family, I could figure out if her mental problems were hereditary."

Brian's face cleared in understanding. "Well, then, you should feel better now, not worse. I know what happened at laMalediction back then was tragic and odd and heavily steeped in voodoo and other old beliefs, but based on my understanding of the events, Marilyn Borque wasn't crazy. You should feel better knowing that."

"If I was a descendant of Marilyn, I would."

Brian's eyes widened. "Oh, hell. You're not saying…"

"It looks like my mother and Wheeler may have shared the same father—a father who descended from Franklin Borque. I don't think Franklin Borque's or Wheeler's mental states were remotely questionable."

Brian's face fell and his shoulders slumped. "I don't know what to say, except that it's still not certain. Based on the diary entries, I agree something wasn't right with Franklin, but Wheeler's issues could have centered around good, old-fashioned greed."

Justine shook her head. "Wheeler believed all that stuff—the prophecy. He kidnapped people and took Olivia hostage. How is that normal, even criminally so?"

"The kidnapping and hostage part was desperation."

"And the other?"

"You don't have to have mental issues to know that something very abnormal is going on at that house. Olivia dreamed about the house and the murder before she'd ever laid eyes on it. Do you think Olivia is crazy?"

"No. I don't know how to explain what Olivia experienced, but it doesn't mean Wheeler was sane."

"And it doesn't mean he wasn't. There are some very sane, very evil people in this world. Are you really going to limit your life, based on supposition?"

"I guess if you put it that way, then, yes, I am. I'm not willing to put someone through the emotional roller coaster I've gone through with my mother."

Brian sighed. "I'm not going to pretend I know everything that's going on in your mother's case, but I've known people with issues. They take medication, watch their diet and they have completely normal lives."

"I know plenty of people live normal lives with mental illness, but you said it yourself, they take medication. Medication worked on my mother at first, but then over time, the effect wore off until it made no difference at all. Every time a new medication came out, the doctors thought it would be the magical cure, but the cure was always temporary. It's not the solution for everyone."

Justine stared down at the counter. Damn, he was as stubborn as she was, and that was saying a lot. She hadn't intended to tell him about the figure in white, but he was essentially insisting on proof of something abnormal before he'd give her fears any credence. "I've seen the figure in white—who I think is Marilyn Borque—aside from that first night."

Brian stared. "You're just saying that to end the argument."

"No. I'm saying it because it's true." She described the white figure she'd seen and how the figure had appeared just as she finished reading the diary passages about the graveyard, then pointed her in the right direction.

Brian listened without interrupting, but when she finished, he shook his head. "I agree that you saw something, but I think when all this shakes out, we'll find a logical explanation for it."

"Like what?"

"I think someone's playing with us."

"You think someone magically knew when I'd read the exact passage in the diaries about the graveyard, then showed up in a white robe and pointed it out? Without leaving footprints…again?"

Justine saw Brian's jaw flex and she knew he wasn't about to give up the fight. "The neighbor, Miss Bergeron, saw something white in the woods right after that rock came through your bedroom window."

"The woman next door? She's probably got cataracts or imagined it."

"I don't think so. She's not young, but I get the impression she doesn't miss much."

Justine threw her hands in the air, completely exhausted. "So what if she did see something? So what if it's a real person and not a ghost? So what if I'm not crazy now? None of that is a guarantee that I'll remain sane forever. I'm sorry, Brian, but this discussion is over."

She slid off the stool and walked down the hall to the bathroom, so tense that every muscle in her body ached. What she needed was a long, hot shower and some space between her and Brian. His argument was persuasive and logical, but she was in no position to gamble. Brian may be able to live with a mentally-ill partner, but that didn't mean Justine could live with the guilt of turning someone's world upside down.

She'd gotten enough answers to satisfy her on her personal pursuit and probably justify a DNA test. Now, she needed to focus every ounce of energy and knowledge she had on finding the emeralds for Olivia so that she could leave Cypriere and forget she'd ever met Brian Marcentel.

BRIAN REMOVED THE PHOTOS from the back sleeve of his notebook and scanned the room, making a mental note of the furniture. The ride to the house had been completely silent and the tension as thick as the morning humidity. The closeness he'd shared with Justine the night before was nowhere in sight; if possible, she was even more closed off now than the first day he'd met her. The whole situation had blown up on him so fast this morning that he still hadn't quite processed it all.

It didn't mean he was being dismissive of Justine's concerns. To be concerned was valid but to permanently limit your life because of it was a self-fulfilling prophecy… There had to be a way to change her mind.

And then what?

He tossed the notebook on the dresser in disgust. Damned good question. He'd been so hell-bent, trying to find a way to convince Justine she was wrong, that he hadn't bothered to come up with a good reason for doing so. He had no way to prove that Justine would live a lonely, miserable life. His sister was single and perfectly happy with the occasional date of her choosing. An archaic belief about marriage hardly applied to today's women, and Justine was definitely a modern woman.

So he was pushing her to let her guard down for what? His feelings for Justine were definitely different than he'd had for other women, but that didn't mean he was ready to promise forever. He ran one hand across the top of his head and blew out a breath. Then why the hell was he pushing her to change the course of her life, when he wasn't even ready to change his own? The only thing he was certain of was that living in such close quarters wasn't going to be easy for either of them.

He took a look at the photos in his hand and tried to refocus his mind on the job at hand. He couldn't solve the problems of Justine Chatry's life, standing in the middle of a dusty bedroom in a derelict old mansion. Justine had requested an hour to do some research before they hiked out to the graveyard to investigate the tunnel in the crypt. It was the only words she'd spoken since leaving the kitchen that morning.

A glance at his watch let him know that a whole seven minutes had passed since they'd entered the house. He'd thought that working upstairs might get his mind off everything else, and maybe it would, if he'd concentrate on the photos and not on Justine. He flipped through the photos until he located the three that depicted the room he stood in.

The bed was featured in the first photo, and checking its placement against the back wall of the room, Brian noticed no difference. But the next photo was a different story. A decorative table that was centered on the side wall in a photo was offset in the room now. Brian double-checked the photo to make sure his visual was right, and frowned. The table was probably a good foot down the wall from where it had been.

Which made absolutely no sense whatsoever, as that table rested on an outside wall of the house. It was the same situation as the bed in the last room he'd checked, but neither the floor nor the wall behind the bed had contained a hiding place for valuables, like he'd thought they might. And now he had a table relocated for no logical or apparent reason, and he wasn't about to buy into the idea that spirits moved them just to get a rise out of him.

He checked the photo again to be certain of the wall space the table used to cover and then pushed the table over a bit more to get clear access to the wall. The wall was covered with a smooth, white plaster, and Brian couldn't detect a break anywhere in the pristine surface. Another dead end. If someone had hidden something in this wall, it had been plastered over, and no one had accessed it since.

So why move the table? It was a decorative item with no drawers or shelves. The kind of thing women put a bowl of dead flowers on or a vase, or both. He peeked underneath but couldn't see a secret panel. No envelope taped to the bottom, like you saw in movies.

Deciding he needed a better look to be completely satisfied, he lifted the table up and placed it upside down on the bed so that he wouldn't scratch the top. He ran his fingers across the bottom, but found nothing to indicate it was anything other than a solid piece of wood. This entire situation was starting to frustrate him. It was like a giant jigsaw puzzle, with the pieces scattered to the wind. None of them made sense individually, and the little sections he'd pieced together didn't seem related.

But something told him that when everything fell into place, the entire picture would contain every single piece and section he'd mentally constructed—Justine's past, the tunnels, the cemetery, the moving furniture, the white figure, Olivia's dreams. All of it was part of one big storm, with laMalediction at its center.

He placed the table back against the wall and made an entry in the notebook that he'd thrown on the dresser. He pulled the rest of the photos from the back of the notebook. That was three rooms already where he'd found furniture out of place. A quick inventory should tell him exactly how mobile the objects in laMalediction had been lately. Maybe if he could identify all the objects that had been moved, he could piece together another section of the puzzle.

Solving the mystery of the moving furniture had to be easier than figuring out how to fit Justine's fractured life into his. Or whether he should even try.

Chapter Eighteen

Justine finished reading the diary entry and placed it on the stack with the others she'd already read. The information was interesting, and somehow it had to be relevant, but for the life of her, she couldn't figure out what it meant. Those pages were specifically removed from the journals and hidden by someone, probably Sissy, who thought they revealed too much, but Marilyn's secrets were still safe, even though Justine had read through all but the last of the entries.

She reached for her bottle of water and took a big drink. Her mind was cluttered with information, about laMalediction, the emeralds, her mother's health, her own impending doom…and Brian. The last was the only one she felt she had any control over, at least in the action department. Her heart had already shifted too much in Brian's direction for her comfort, but that didn't mean her responsibilities ended. If anything, the fact that she cared for him created even more responsibility for her, to protect him from a future of watching and waiting for the disease to take over.

Which put her right back to her original plan—find the emeralds and get the heck out of Cypriere. Sighing, she picked up the second-to-last page of diary entries, hoping it would provide a clue to the location of the cursed jewels. Her pulse quickened as she read Sissy's words.

August 19, 1862
It has been many months since I was able to visit my cousin, and she was dismayed to learn of Marilyn's actions. Bringing her lover here was risky enough, but I suppose it was worth it, as he succumbed to the fever. If Marilyn hadn't sent for him, she might never have seen him again. Her happiness those few weeks was something I'd never seen in her.

My cousin told me no good would come from summoning the child. That the dead would follow the living into Marilyn's womb and enter this house at the birth. That the door opened that night would forever link all descendants of Marilyn to the past and to the other side.

What the hell? Justine reread the passage to make sure she hadn't misunderstood—that Sissy was saying Marilyn had used voodoo to create her pregnancy with a dead man. In all of her mother's ramblings, Justine had never heard anything that outlandish. It couldn't possibly be true, but apparently Sissy believed it, as did her cousin.

Surely, Marilyn was pregnant before her lover died. The ceremony in the graveyard was just a coincidence. Marilyn could not have possibly summoned a fertilized embryo into her womb. It amazed her that anyone—even someone grounded in the old beliefs—could think such a thing possible, but clearly Sissy did. No wonder a negative tone hung over this house. Even something as joyful as the conception of a child was all hidden in secrecy and fear.

Justine needed to find the lover's grave. Marilyn would

have trusted her lover's spirit to protect her secrets. A clue to the missing emeralds might be contained at the gravesite. She checked the time on her laptop and realized the hour she'd asked Brian to give her was up.

Just as she closed her laptop, he knocked on the library door and stepped inside. "Are you ready to go?"

"Sure, but before we check the tunnel, I need to find a grave." She explained the diary passage and her thought on the lover's grave, then passed the diary page over to him to read.

Her description drew no visible response whatsoever from Brian, even when she explained divining a baby from a dead man, nor did his expression change as he read the diary entry. Either he was mad or he was respecting her wishes and had put up his own wall.

His detachment should have been a relief, but Justine felt a wave of disappointment pass over her that he was giving up so easily. Which was foolish. They'd spent one night together. It was hardly the basis for an attachment worth fighting for. Unfortunately, no one had explained that to her heart, or ego, or whatever was inside her that caused that feeling that she'd lost something important.

"That's fine," Brian said. "I also want to check the outside perimeter of the graveyard for another path or road. If someone was using the graveyard tunnel to gain entry into the house, there has to be another access point."

"That makes sense. Are you ready to go?"

"Sure." He handed the page back to her. "Oh, man. I'm sorry. My hands must be dirty from moving furniture and I smeared some on the page."

Justine glanced at the brown smudges as she placed the entry in a pile with the others. "It's no big deal. I don't think the documents have any historical value except to the family, and maybe not even then. I doubt Olivia is any more interested in carrying this past around with her than I am."

"I'm sure you're right," he said. "Let me go wash my hands and we'll go. I'll meet you out front." He turned and left the room without so much as a backward glance.

Justine sighed and hoped for the millionth time that morning that she found the emeralds soon.

AFTER A FULL HOUR of thrashing in the underbrush, Brian spotted the path behind the graveyard. He bent down and picked up a piece of dirt from the tire track on the ground. "It's recent," he said.

"What kind of tire made that?" Justine asked.

"ATV—a four-wheeler."

"Where do you think the path goes? Do you think it connects with the one behind the caretaker's cottage?"

"It may. Or it may continue to a road large enough for a vehicle. Either way, someone would have an opportunity to come and go without having to use the main road."

"Someone who owned one of those cabins or knew about an alternate road," Justine pointed out.

"Or someone who borrowed a cabin on a regular basis." Brian blew out a breath. "I wish the sheriff hadn't interrupted my conversation with Tom Breaux. I might have found out who owned those other cabins."

"Maybe it's been Tom all along, and he's trying to throw you off. He might have seen John and Olivia that day when they snuck up behind the cabins. I get the feeling he's smarter than he's letting on."

"He's ex-military and he's seen action. You don't get through that by not noticing things. Whether he's involved, I don't know. Seems a strange time to sell the cabin, if he was using it for nefarious reasons, but then I only have his word that he sold it to begin with." Brian shook his head.

"We don't have time to follow this road today. I want to get a look at that tunnel, and we still need to find that grave first."

It took another exasperating thirty minutes to locate the grave.

"This is it," Justine said and pointed to a single grave in the section with Sissy's family. The headstone was a simple slab of granite with no fancy adornments.

"How can you be sure?"

"The eye engraved at the top of the tombstone. It's supposed to give the dead the ability to see into the realm of the living. All the rest of Sissy's family have the magnolia on their tombstones. It was probably the family symbol."

Brian looked at the creepy eye on the top of the tombstone and shook his head. "I guess that makes as much sense as anything else. So if the emeralds were here, where would they be?"

Justine studied the tombstone and frowned. "I think if they were actually around the grave, Wheeler would have found them, but I was hoping to find something…a clue. Anything that gave me a direction to look in."

Brian leaned over to study some markings down the side of the tombstone that appeared as if they'd been scratched into the granite after it was in place. "What are these markings here on the side?"

Justine stepped closer to the tombstone and leaned over to inspect the etchings Brian had indicated. Her bare arm brushed against Brian's and she mentally cursed her body when her skin began to tingle. She shifted just enough so that their bodies no longer touched, and studied the scratches. "It's uniform, which means it's deliberate, but I can't tell exactly what it is. Teardrops maybe? It looks like a line of teardrops down the side of the tombstone."

"Maybe Marilyn did it. Her tears for her lost love."

Justine felt her heart catch in her throat. The thought was so sad but so beautiful. She ran one finger down the row of tears and willed her own to stay at bay. It was hard enough to live life denying yourself what you wanted, but Marilyn had it and had lost it. Tragically so.

"I don't think there's anything here that can help me," Justine said.

Brian nodded and pointed to the gray clouds moving over the swamp. "We'd better get moving on to the tunnel. I don't want to be caught out here in a storm."

Justine glanced up at the sky then nodded. She didn't want to be caught out in a storm, either.

They accessed the crypt and Brian pressed the trigger to open the panel that hid the tunnel. He handed Justine a flashlight from his backpack and grabbed a spotlight for himself. Justine couldn't help but notice that he'd also tucked his pistol in the waistband of his jeans. He'd probably noticed her pistol tucked in her jeans under her hooded jacket, but he hadn't commented.

Brian stepped into the tunnel and started feeling the inside wall. "I want to figure out how to open the door from the inside. I think I found it."

Justine nodded as the door slid silently into place, then reopened a couple of seconds later. "Good thinking."

"I'm going to go in first. We'll move slowly and check the tunnel as we go. Stop me if you see any sign of an offshoot or a hidden door. If I stop short, stop with me and be very quiet. That means I've heard something I need to identify. Any questions?"

Justine shook her head. He'd rattled off the instructions like a military mission. Given the secret tunnels and an unknown enemy, she supposed the situation might share similarities to what he'd experienced at war.

He stared at her for a moment as if he wanted to say

something more, but then he whirled around and entered the tunnel, glancing back only briefly to make sure she was following. The stairs down from the crypt were wide but steep. Justine made sure she took deliberate steps, checking each stone step before placing her foot upon it. The last thing they needed was for one of them to have an accident.

It probably only took a minute, but it seemed like far longer before Justine stepped off the last step and into the tunnel below. Like the stairwell, it was wide, but the low ceiling gave it more of a closed-in feel. No light penetrated from the stairwell and Justine was grateful for the spotlight Brian carried that illuminated the long stretch of tunnel before them.

"Can you see an end?" Justine asked as she stepped beside him.

"No. It looks like a straight shot into darkness."

"Sounds inviting."

"Yeah. Well, let's get this over with." He shined the spotlight down on the stretch of ground directly in front of them, then lifted it back up and started down the tunnel. They moved slowly, inspecting the walls visually and with their hands as they progressed, looking for any indication of another tunnel, a hidden room or an exit.

Finally, they reached a turn in the tunnel and Brian stopped, directing his spotlight first at the tunnel behind them, then again at the stretch after the bend. Justine checked her watch. "We've been walking down here almost twenty minutes. How far do you think we've come?"

"A half mile maybe. It looks like this stretch is shorter though. I see a wall about twenty yards ahead."

"Probably just another turn. We'll probably exit this tunnel somewhere in Mexico."

"Ha. I don't think we've traveled that far, and we've

been moving steadily west, which is good. That put us back in the direction of the house."

"I haven't seen any indication of a hidden wall."

"I haven't, either. This tunnel may be just a passageway from the graveyard to somewhere else on the estate. The hidden rooms may all be contained directly below laMal-ediction. You ready for the next leg?"

"Absolutely. I can't wait to find out where this tunnel comes out. The amount of work that went into this and all the secret passageways and rooms is staggering. Franklin Borque was one paranoid guy."

"With good reason. When you're a monster, there will always be someone out to get you." Brian directed his spot-light down the second leg of tunnel and started walking.

Justine clutched her flashlight and followed behind, the word *monster* still echoing through her mind. It was such a simple word, but so complex when attached to a human. Unfortunately, it was very applicable in this case.

She walked behind Brian and held in a sigh of disap-pointment. So far, this excursion had yielded nothing but a road that led somewhere away from the graveyard, a grave with no discernible clue to the location of the emeralds and a tunnel that went somewhere as yet to be determined. She hoped the end of the tunnel provided something for them to work from. Otherwise, they were back at square one.

Lost in thought, Justine didn't realize Brian had stopped until she ran smack into him. "Sorry," she said as she backed up a step.

"Looks like the end of the line."

Justine peered around the bend in the tunnel and saw a set of stone steps leading up. "Do you think it leads to the basement of laMalediction?"

"Maybe, but I didn't feel like we were getting lower in

the tunnel. We would have had to for the basement to be above us."

Justine shook her head. "You've got a much better sense of placement than I do. I have no idea whether or not the tunnel drifted down."

"Well, let's see." He passed Justine his spotlight and pulled his pistol from the waistband of his jeans. "Just in case."

Justine gripped the spotlight and watched as Brian inched up the stairs and searched for a switch to open a door at the top. She heard a faint click and the ceiling above Brian slid silently back. Brian paused for a couple of seconds and Justine knew he was listening for any sound of movement. Her heart beat so loudly, she was afraid he could hear it.

He poked his head through the opening. "I'll be damned," he said and continued up the stairs through the opening. "Come on up. It's safe."

Justine climbed the stairs and crawled out of the opening, then stared in surprise at Brian, who was kneeling at the edge of the dining table right smack in the middle of laMalediction's kitchen. She looked up at the top of the table that rested just inches from her head.

"You've got to be kidding me," she said. "We sat right here with that beneath us and never knew?"

Brian shook his head. "And with the table over it, no one would walk on it and hear the difference in the sound of the flooring. My security system must have been a real source of amusement to the intruder."

"Wow," Justine said, and started to crawl out from under the table.

"Hold on and I'll move it so you can stand."

"It will be too heavy—" She cut short as Brian effortlessly slid the enormous table across the kitchen floor. She rose from her stooped position and stared at the table.

"What's wrong?"

"You moved the table so easily. Is it heavy?"

"Not really."

Justine frowned and stepped up to the table, then gripped the edge with both hands and pulled. The table slid easily across the floor toward her. "This should be heavier. It almost feels like..."

She bent down and looked underneath the table again, studying the corners where the thick, ornate legs connected with the top. In one corner, the wood appeared a little darker than the rest of the table. She ran one finger across the dark spot and stared down at the brown stain on her finger.

"What did you find?" Brian asked as she rose.

She smelled her finger and showed it to Brian. "Wood stain. This table has had a coat of it in the last couple of weeks. With the humidity so high, it still hasn't dried completely in the corners."

"Why would anyone restain an antique?"

"It's not an antique." Justine stared at Brian, her mind whirling to put all the pieces together. "It all makes sense now." She grabbed Brian's arm, her excitement rising.

"Don't you see?" she asked. "I banged my leg on this table earlier this week and it didn't budge, and you said the furniture upstairs had been moved but wasn't hiding anything. Then you got that brown stain on the diary entry after you'd been working with the furniture upstairs."

Brian's face cleared in understanding. "You think someone's been stealing the antiques and replacing them with copies. How lucrative could that possibly be?"

"Very, given the quality and age of the assets in this house. Hundreds of thousands of dollars if you cleaned out every room, and who knows what's stored in the basement and attic. Someone could spend years replicating the furniture and selling the originals, and no one would have been the wiser."

"The tunnel under the table is wide enough to have moved a lot of it out that way, leaving only the big pieces for when the caretaker was absent."

"Locals would know the caretaker's schedule and hear about any other scheduled departures from Cypriere. There's no hardware store here to speak of."

"No. It was a forty-five-minute drive to the closest one."

"Easily leaving a two-to-three-hour window of opportunity to remove larger items."

"And you're certain this is a phony?"

"Of course. It was part of my studies, and I've contributed to books on antiques."

"Which anyone who was keeping tabs on you would know," Brian said, his voice elevating in excitement. "That's why he wants to get rid of you, Justine. You can identify the fake antiques. When Olivia left, he probably thought he was home free—until you showed up and presented an even bigger problem than Olivia. No one but myself, Olivia and John, and the estate attorney know you're here to find the emeralds. He probably assumed you were here to catalog everything for sale."

Justine stared at him. "Oh, man! I literally said that was the reason I was here that first time we went to the café. I thought I was being smart hiding the real reason I was here, and instead, I said the one thing that would set him off the most."

"Do you mind taking a look at some of the furniture upstairs that was out of place? I want to be sure before I contact John and Olivia."

"Absolutely," Justine said, and followed Brian out of the kitchen, elated at the revelation.

There *was* a simple explanation for everything happening at laMalediction. A criminal one, but simple. Just as Brian had suggested.

IT DIDN'T TAKE MUCH effort for Justine to identify several pieces that were fakes. Cleverly and carefully constructed fakes, but fakes nonetheless. Brian's excitement was almost contagious as they moved from room to room, with Justine identifying the pieces that had been replaced. He made notes on the back of photos and Justine could just see the wheels spinning in his mind. Probably mentally running through how to locate the stolen property and identify the seller—a task he was far more suited to than chasing ghosts or uncovering old mysteries shrouded in voodoo lore.

They were so engrossed in their task that they never noticed a storm moving in, until a huge burst of lightning flashed outside the bedroom window, followed by an earsplitting boom of thunder. Justine jumped at the blast and looked out the window that overlooked the courtyard. "Should we make a run for it?"

Brian moved next to her and looked outside, frowning. "I don't think so. It wasn't supposed to rain at all today. Maybe this will be over quickly."

Justine stared at the sheet of rain falling across the courtyard and hoped he was right. She didn't relish the thought of being caught in laMalediction for the night.

"You'd think, with all the rain, that fountain would be a small swamp, but it's always dry." Justine pointed to the huge fountain in the center of the courtyard.

"It must have a leak. It's not grown over much, though,

so it's probably recent. The water would have protected it from weeds pushing through from the sides or bottom."

The water would have protected it...

Brian's word faded away as Justine stared at the fountain.

Water, water everywhere. Her mother's words flashed through her mind.

The marks on the tombstone. They weren't tears—they were drops of water. In an instant, Justine knew the answer she'd been searching for. "The fountain! The emeralds are hidden in the fountain."

She ran out of the bedroom, dashed down the stairs and out into the blinding rain.

Chapter Nineteen

Brian didn't even have time to process Justine's words, much less reply, before she'd run out of the room as if on fire. He heard the front door slam as he hurried down the stairs to the front entry. He opened the front door and a wave of rain blew onto him, stinging his skin. The wind whipped through the entry like a tornado and he had to squint to make out Justine in the storm.

He could see her crouched in the middle of the fountain, seemingly oblivious to the blinding storm that raged around her. Brian shook his head. She was either going to get struck by lightning or drown. He hurried to the library to grab the raincoat she hadn't bothered to grab before running outside, intending to make a dash to give it to her. But as he turned to leave, something outside the library window caught his eye.

He stepped up to the window, straining to make out the moving object, and his breath caught in his throat when he realized that the white-robed figure was moving across the courtyard, directly at Justine. He pounded on the library window but there was no way Justine could hear him over the storm. Pulling his pistol from his waistband, he ran down the hall and out of the house into the storm.

Justine was squatting down at the front of the fountain, her back to the white figure that approached her. Brian yelled as he rushed out the door, but the white figure was closing in fast. Justine looked up at him when he yelled, a startled expression on her face. She whirled around just as the white figure reached the fountain and lifted one arm.

Brian saw the flash of steel and yelled again. Justine turned to run but lost her footing and crashed to the ground. The white figure ran straight at Justine, the knife flashing above the hooded head. Before the attacker reached Justine, Brian took aim and fired while running.

The bullet caught the attacker in the shoulder and he dropped his knife. He scrambled to recover it, but Brian tackled him before he reached it. Justine rushed around the side of the center feature and grabbed the knife from the bottom of the fountain.

The attacker's body was limp and he didn't struggle at all as Brian turned him over. He pulled the white hood back from his face and stared in shock at the unconscious face of the café waitress, Deedee. Justine sucked in a breath and he looked up at her.

"Why? I don't get it," Justine said.

"I don't either, but let's get her out of the storm until she comes around. Then I've got some questions."

Justine nodded, then yelled, "Wait! The emeralds. I had just loosened a tile etched with the same raindrops as the tombstone."

She bent down and worked off a piece of loose tile from the base of the fountain. The two stones tumbled out of their hiding place and into her hand. Justine stared in amazement at the emeralds, still glittering despite being covered with decades of dirt and with copper twined around it. She closed her hand around them and hurried to the estate. Brian followed close behind, carrying Deedee.

JUSTINE WATCHED the unconscious Deedee lying on the couch in the sitting room, as Brian rushed to the bathroom for towels and medical supplies. A million questions ran through Justine's mind as she stared down at the white-robed figure. Of all the things Justine had suspected, Deedee being her stalker wasn't one of them, and she was anxious for answers.

Deedee stirred a bit and Justine sat down on the coffee table in front of her. The waitress opened her eyes and looked around then bolted up when she saw Justine, her expression one of complete panic. "I had to stop you. You were going to free the spirits."

Justine frowned. What in the world… Then she remembered the emeralds. She unfolded her hand and showed the stones to Deedee. The waitress paled and she scurried to the far corner of the couch, wrapping her arms around her knees in a fetal position.

"No!" Deedee wailed. "What have you done? We'll all die now, just like he said."

Justine felt her heart drop as she looked into the young woman's eyes. She might as well have been looking at her mother. Deedee may have been stalking her, but someone had put those ideas into an already damaged mind. Someone who knew her well enough to know how easily she could be manipulated.

Someone with a lot of antique furniture to steal.

"Who told you about the spirits, Deedee? Was it Tom?"

"No. Tom warned me never to come here, but *he* said I had to keep you away. *He* said you would ruin everything."

"Who? Who told you to try and scare me away?"

Deedee shook her head. "He said he'd kill me if I told our secret."

Justine struggled for patience. knowing more than anyone that she wouldn't be able to force the information out of Deedee in the mental state she was in. She was already too paranoid—too psychotic. "Let's play a game. He didn't say anything about playing games, right?"

Deedee stared at her for a couple of seconds, the uncertainty and suspicion on her face clear as day. "What kind of game?"

"I'll ask a question and you answer yes or no. That way, you never say a name. Okay?"

Deedee didn't look convinced, but she nodded.

"Is the man from Cypriere?"

"Yes."

"Have I met the man?"

"Yes."

Justine stared at the waitress. She'd been expecting her to say no. The only man she'd met in Cypriere was Tom, but Deedee had already said the bad guy wasn't Tom. It hit her like lightning and she sucked in a breath.

"Is the man Sheriff Blanchard?"

Deedee didn't even have to answer. The fear on her face said it all.

A million thoughts ran through Justine's mind as all of the pieces fell into place. The one person who could access the estate under the guise of "checking things out" that wouldn't raise an eyebrow on the old caretaker. The one person who never managed to find the vandals and hoodlums he claimed were causing the trouble. The one person who had access to the police database and could break her identity if he wanted to.

Suddenly Deedee's eyes opened wide and her hands started shaking as she stared over Justine's shoulder toward the door to the kitchen. The tunnel!

Justine knew he was standing behind her before she ever turned around.

"Sheriff," Justine acknowledged as she turned to face the man.

Brian heard voices coming from the sitting room as soon as he stepped onto the upstairs landing. He could hear Justine trying to coax information out of Deedee, so he crept slowly and quietly down the stairwell, afraid that Deedee would clam up if she heard him coming. He hung on to every word and stopped walking down the stairs completely when he heard Justine ask about Sheriff Blanchard.

He waited several seconds for a reply, but none came. Then he heard Justine utter the single word "Sheriff"—not as a question, but as a greeting, and Brian felt his blood run cold. While they'd been inspecting furniture and finding the emeralds, the sheriff could have easily entered the house through the tunnel and waited for them in case his plan to use Deedee didn't work.

Now he had Justine and Deedee trapped in the sitting room and Brian had no doubt he had his pistol trained on them. He crept silently down the remaining steps and slipped to the back of the entryway and into the hall, trying to determine the best course of action.

Sheriff Blanchard had entered the sitting room from the kitchen, or Brian would have spotted him, so entering the sitting room from the front entry of the house would put him in full view of the man. The best plan was to sneak down the hall and into the kitchen, hope to catch him from behind and hope to hell the floors didn't creak as he made his way.

He slipped silently down the hallway, careful to tread on the carpet runner down the center of the wooden floor. He stopped just outside the kitchen entry, trying to determine where Sheriff Blanchard stood. He heard movement, but couldn't determine whether the sheriff had stepped into the sitting room or was still standing in the entry between the kitchen and sitting room.

Just as he was about to move, Sheriff Blanchard spoke and Brian froze.

"You should have taken my warnings from the beginning," Sheriff Blanchard said. "Being stubborn is only going to get you dead."

"You thought you'd scare me, having Deedee pose as a ghost?" Justine asked. "Why would you think I'd fall for that?"

"Your mother believed in all of it. I assumed you were brought up on the same stories. How was I to know you were a 'modern' woman with different ideas?"

"You might have gotten a clue when I didn't bolt the first night, but then you're not all that quick on the uptake, are you?"

Brian tensed at Justine's harsh words, and knew he had to make a move. It was almost as if she was intentionally provoking him—but why? He inched closer to the doorway and stuck his head in the kitchen, relieved to see the sheriff standing just inside the entryway to the sitting room with his back to the kitchen. Brian lifted his pistol into position and started for a moment when movement in the kitchen caught his eye.

He stared across the room and realized the light from the hall behind him had cast his shadow on the back of the kitchen wall. That's what he'd seen.

And what Justine could see if she was facing the sheriff.

That explained why she was intentionally goading the man. She knew Brian was in the kitchen, and was trying to keep the sheriff's focus on her so that Brian could make a move. If she could just distract him for a bit longer, he'd be able to slip into the kitchen and come up behind him.

"Why go to all this trouble over furniture?" Justine asked. "Is it really worth killing people?"

The sheriff laughed. "I have over three hundred thousand dollars in an offshore account collecting interest, thanks to the furniture in this house. And when I sell those emeralds you're holding, it will be the icing on my retirement cake. Between the furniture money and my police retirement, I would have had enough money to live in luxury the rest of my life. If only that meddling Olivia could have waited one more year to visit here. All of this could have been avoided."

"I'm so sorry two women doing their jobs interfered with your crime spree. You won't get away with this, you know. Any expert will spot the fakes and the police will search for the original furniture. It's only a matter of time until they track it back to you."

"And thanks to those emeralds, I'll be long gone before that happens."

Brian tightened his grip on his pistol and slipped around the doorway and into the kitchen. Only three steps and he'd be right behind the sheriff.

"You may get away from here," Justine said, "but you'll still pay. I do believe in some of the old ways, and you have a cosmic reckoning coming to you for using Deedee the way you did. You knew her mind wasn't stable, and you took advantage of her."

Sheriff Blanchard laughed. "I guess you would know about Deedee's unstable mind. She is your sister, after all."

Brian heard the sharp intake of breath from Justine and knew he had to move quickly. That statement had put her off balance. But just as he stepped behind Sheriff Blanchard, Deedee caught sight of him and screamed. Sheriff Blanchard whirled around, knocking his gun from his hand, but before the sheriff could fire a shot at Brian, Justine hit him from behind and sent both of them sprawling onto the kitchen floor.

Brian leaped for his pistol at the same time Sheriff Blanchard reached for his own, just inches away. As the sheriff's fingers closed around the hilt of the pistol, Brian leveled his gun directly at the sheriff's head. "It's over," Brian said.

Sheriff Blanchard stared at him, and for a moment Brian thought the man was going to go for it. Then he released the pistol and slumped down on the kitchen floor, finally beaten. Brian retrieved the sheriff's gun and secured his hands behind his back with his belt. Then Brian extended his hand to a clearly stunned Justine to help her up from the floor. "Are you all right?"

Justine threw her arms around him and squeezed him tight. Surprised, Brian wrapped his free arm around her and held her close to him, feeling her heart pounding against his chest.

"You were right." Justine looked up at him, tears spilling over onto her cheeks. "When faced with the possibility of my life ending, I realized how much living I have to do. Our night together wasn't a mistake. It was the best night of my life."

Brian stared at Justine, stunned. "Are you saying…?"

"I'm saying that, if you're willing to take a chance, then so am I. I know we've sorta jumped the gun and skipped right to the sex part, but I was thinking maybe we could start with a date."

Brian wanted to believe her, but so much had happened

in just the past hour that Justine needed to process. "What about Deedee?"

Justine frowned. "I don't know if there's any truth to what he said, but I'll do my best to find out."

"And if Deedee is your sister?"

"I'll get her a lawyer and see that she gets the help she needs."

Brian lowered his lips to Justine's for a soft kiss. That was all he needed to hear.

Epilogue

One month later

Justine sat next to Brian at the restaurant table, looking across at Olivia and John, who still sparkled with newlywed bliss. Brian squeezed her hand under the table and she smiled, knowing he felt as good about life right now as she did. They'd been dating since the showdown at laMalediction, and although they didn't spend time together every day, they talked often and extensively on the phone. Justine knew her heart belonged to Brian and she knew he felt the same way. They'd spent the past weekend looking at houses to rent in a small town just outside of New Orleans, and not even once had Justine had second thoughts.

"It's official," John said as he scanned a text message on his phone. "Fish and wildlife picked up that mechanic, Chris Pauley, for poaching alligators on the estate. That explains why Tom saw him there and where he got the money to buy the cabin."

Brian shook his head. "I knew that guy was up to something. Alligator poaching. That's a new one for me."

Olivia laughed. "That's *really* a new one for me." She looked across the table at Justine. "How's your mother?"

"Declining rapidly," Justine replied, "but she's not in

pain, and I've been expecting this for a long time. I'm prepared. And she deserves a rest."

Olivia reached across the table and placed her hand on Justine's. The obvious concern in her expression warmed Justine's heart, making her thankful all over again for her new family.

"I am so sorry, Justine. What about Deedee?"

"According to the DNA kits, we share the same mother, but not the same father. Unfortunately, I haven't been able to find any more information on Deedee's father than my own, so it will likely remain a mystery. She experienced a complete psychotic break after what happened, and she's been remanded to the state mental facility. She'll finally get the care she needs."

Olivia gave her hand a squeeze and reached for her wineglass. "Sheriff Blanchard confessed to leaving you those notes, just like we suspected. With Sheriff Blanchard on his way to a long prison term and laMalediction being transformed into a halfway house with the oil money, I'd say our work here is done."

"No more dreams?" Justine asked.

"Not a one since the day you found the emeralds." Olivia frowned.

"I got a letter from Tom Breaux last week," Justine said. "He has a theory on everything that happened."

"Really?" John said. "This ought to be good."

Justine smiled. "He thinks that when the crack in the fountain allowed the water to leave, the binding on the emeralds lifted and allowed the bad spirits to return to claim laMalediction. He thinks the stones called to you and me, given our relationship to the Borques."

Olivia sighed her head. "Even though he knows Deedee was the figure in white?"

"That's the interesting thing. Both times I saw the figure, Deedee was working in the café. She was doing inventory late that first night we arrived at the estate, and she was waiting tables the day the figure pointed me to the graveyard."

"Seriously?" Olivia said. "Then what…?"

Justine shrugged. "I don't pretend to understand any of the things that happened at laMalediction—in the past or in the present—but I like to think that somewhere out there is a force larger than any of us. It just had unfinished business."

Olivia smiled and lifted her wineglass. "To *finished* business, then."

"Absolutely," Justine said and leaned over to kiss Brian before lifting her glass.

* * * * *

COMING NEXT MONTH

Available August 9, 2011

#1293 SOVEREIGN SHERIFF
Cowboys Royale
Cassie Miles

#1294 STAMPEDED
Whitehorse, Montana: Chisholm Cattle Company
B.J. Daniels

#1295 FLASHBACK
Gayle Wilson

#1296 PROTECTING THE PREGNANT WITNESS
The Precinct: SWAT
Julie Miller

#1297 LOCKED AND LOADED
Mystery Men
HelenKay Dimon

#1298 DAKOTA MARSHAL
Jenna Ryan

Once bitten, twice shy. That's Gabby Wade's motto—especially when it comes to Adamson men. And the moment she meets Jon Adamson her theory is confirmed. But with each encounter a little something *sparks between them, making her wonder if she's been too hasty to dismiss this one!*

Enjoy this sneak peek from ONE GOOD REASON by Sarah Mayberry, available August 2011 from Harlequin® Superromance®.

Gabby Wade's heartbeat thumped in her ears as she marched to her office. She wanted to pretend it was because of her brisk pace returning from the file room, but she wasn't that good a liar.

Her heart was beating like a tom-tom because Jon Adamson had touched her. In a very male, very possessive way. She could still feel the heat of his big hand burning through the seat of her khakis as he'd steadied her on the ladder.

It had taken every ounce of self-control to tell him to unhand her. What she'd really wanted was to grab him by his shirt and, well, explore all those urges his touch had instantly brought to life.

While she might not like him, she was wise enough to understand that it wasn't always about liking the other person. Sometimes it was about pure animal attraction.

Refusing to think about it, she turned to work. When she'd typed in the wrong figures three times, Gabby admitted she was too tired and too distracted. Time to call it a day.

As she was leaving, she spied Jon at his workbench in the shop. His head was propped on his hand as he studied blueprints. It wasn't until she got closer that she saw his

HSREXP0811I

eyes were shut.

He looked oddly boyish. There was something innocent and unguarded in his expression. She felt a weakening in her resistance to him.

"Jon." She put her hand on his shoulder, intending to shake him awake. Instead, it rested there like a caress.

His eyes snapped open.

"You were asleep."

"No, I was, uh, visualizing something on this design." He gestured to the blueprint in front of him then rubbed his eyes.

That gesture dealt a bigger blow to her resistance. She realized it wasn't only animal attraction pulling them together. She took a step backward as if to get away from the knowledge.

She cleared her throat. "I'm heading off now."

He gave her a smile, and she could see his exhaustion.

"Yeah, I should, too." He stood and stretched. The hem of his T-shirt rose as he arched his back and she caught a flash of hard male belly. She looked away, but it was too late. Her mind had committed the image to permanent memory.

And suddenly she knew, for good or bad, she'd never look at Jon the same way again.

Find out what happens next in ONE GOOD REASON, available August 2011 from Harlequin® Superromance®!

HSREXP0811

MYSTERY UNRAVELED

Find the answers to the puzzles in last month's INTRIGUE titles!

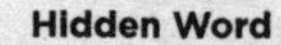

Hidden Word
(Writing & Computers)

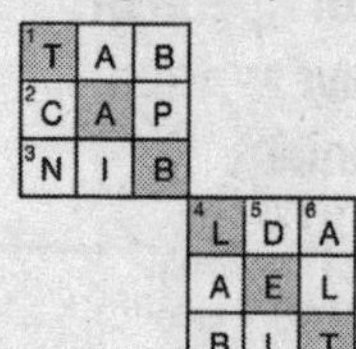

Hidden Word: TABLET

Hidden Word
(House)

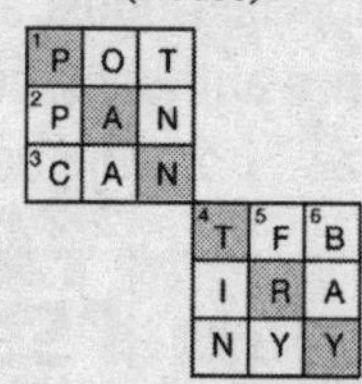

Hidden Word: PANTRY

Figure Counting
(Squares & Rectangles)

Thirty-eight

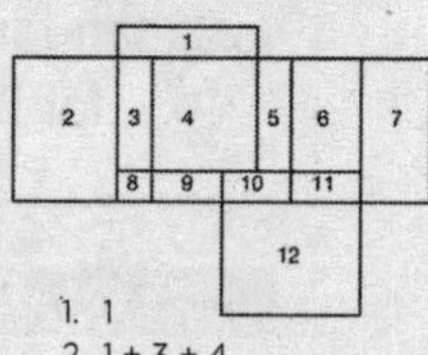

1. 1
2. 1 + 3 + 4

Figure Counting
(Triangles)

Eight

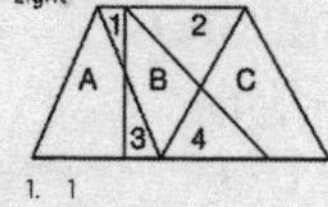

1. 1
2. 2
3. 3
4. 4
5. A (3 as a part)
6. B (3 and 4 as parts)
7. B (1 and 2 as parts)
8. C (4 as a part)

Matchstick Puzzle
(12-Matchstick Arrangement)

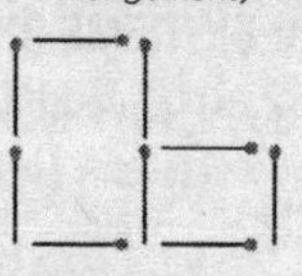

Matchstick Puzzle
(20-Matchstick Arrangement)

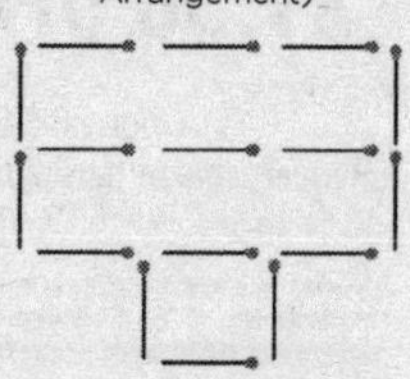